HENRY VON STRAY in
A CASEBOOK OF CRIME

THRILLING ADVENTURES OF SUSPENSE FROM THE GOLDEN AGE OF MYSTERY

HENRY VON STRAY IN
A CASEBOOK OF CRIME

THRILLING ADVENTURES OF SUSPENSE FROM THE GOLDEN AGE OF MYSTERY

VOLUME ONE

ANDREW & JOHN MCALEER

First published by Level Best Books/Historia 2025

This novel is entirely a work of fiction. The names, characters and incidents portrayed in it are the work of the author's imagination. Any resemblance to actual persons, living or dead, events or localities is entirely coincidental.

Andrew and John McAleer assert the moral right to be identified as the author of this work.

Author Photo Credit: Ruth Delaney McAleer

First edition

ISBN: 978-1-68512-894-4

Cover art by Level Best Designs

*This book was professionally typeset on Reedsy.
Find out more at reedsy.com*

For Clifford McElroy Friend, Educator, Philanthropist, Boston College Science Librarian

Contents

Praise for the Henry von Stray Series

& Edgar Award Winner John McAleer

"Recovering the first [von Stray] story was a brilliant find, but continuing the series reveals a different kind of brilliance. More than mimicry or some elevated form of pastiche, these von Stray stories—one by John McAleer, three now by Andrew—strike me as true collaborations, the father as a young boy and son as a grown man speaking with one shining voice."—Edgar winner Art Taylor (From the Introduction to *A Casebook of Crime*)

"Andrew McAleer's light-hearted Henry von Stray extravaganzas give fresh life to characters first created by his Edgar-winning father John more than eighty-five years ago—quite something!"—Martin Edwards, Diamond Dagger recipient, Edgar Award-winner, President of the Detection Club

"Von Stray lives on! Fans and aficionados of Golden Age detective fiction are in for a real treat with this unique anthology from Edgar Allan Poe award winner, the late John McAleer *and* his award-winning son Andrew featuring the intrepid private detective Henry von Stray and his jaunty sidekick Professor John Dilpate. What makes this collection so exciting is that Andrew has taken up his father's mantle and continued the von Stray legacy, flawlessly capturing the style, tone, and essence of the original with a seamless transition. McAleer has infused new life into the legendary sleuthing duo with the trademark wit, clever puzzles, and plot twists that are so deliciously satisfying. Even better, we're told there are more von Stray adventures to come. I just can't wait."—Hannah Dennison, author of The Honeychurch Hall Mysteries Series

"*A Casebook of Crime* is the ultimate treat for mystery readers—a McAleer father-and-son collaboration of four brilliant, authentic mysteries from another era. Every Henry von Stray story is witty, clever, and—above all—entertaining. I loved this book!"—John M. Floyd, Shamus- and Derringer Award-winning author

"John McAleer's classic detective Henry von Stray is *truly* fun, an entertaining revisit to mystery stories of another era. Inventively written, in a solid, energetic style. Witty, classic and far too long kept secreted away."—Tom Sawyer, bestselling novelist, screenwriter, playwright, Showrunner/Head Writer of *Murder, She Wrote*

"These lively Henry von Stray tales will delight fans of traditional mysteries and Sherlockian puzzles!"—Lia Matera, Shamus Award-winning author of the Willa Jansson novels

"Sherlock Holmes and Hercule Poirot fans will thoroughly enjoy the thrilling adventures of Edgar winner John McAleer's Golden Age detective Henry von Stray and his trusted companion Professor John Dilpate."—Gay Toltl Kinman, Agatha Award finalist

"John McAleer's 'Case of the Illustrious Banker'...is just one of the treasures unearthed...in *Edgar & Shamus Go Golden*."—Midwest Book Review

"Sit back and savour original mystery tales written exclusively by Edgar Allan Poe and Shamus Award-winning authors... In something of a coup John McAleer's 'The Case of the Illustrious Banker' makes it debut more than 80 years since it was written, and 40 years before he won an Edgar Award."—Crime Fiction Lover

"...shimmering with cleverness and whimsey."—*The Washington Post*

"[A]stonishing setting and fine feeling—tasteful beyond belief."—*Chicago Tribune*

"Humorous, erudite, a good puzzle and a good read. When you turn the last page, you'll feel as though your ancestors were born in Boston."—Mary Higgins Clark

"A crackerjack mystery. Witty, with genuine, authentic atmosphere."—*The Book World*

"A delicious mystery that combines the best of *The Proper Bostonians* with the best of Parker's Spenser stories."—Robin Moore, NY Times #1 bestselling author of *The French Connection*

"John McAleer is right on target—*Coign of Vantage* is a pleasure."—Robert B. Parker

"John McAleer's *Coign of Vantage* should please mystery lovers on several levels. This is also a book for lovers of sophisticated dialogue, fanciers of libraries and bookish matters, and those who appreciate their tales laced with romance, satire, and wit."—*Alfred Hitchcock's Mystery Magazine*

"John McAleer has done more than justice to recording the several stages of Rex Stout's life. He portrays a life every bit as engrossing as a Nero Wolfe mystery. The full flavor of Stout's wit and urbanity comes through."—*Washington Post*

"McAleer's biography will cause all admirers of Wolfe and Archie to rise in tribute to this remarkable man. Stout could not be in better hands."—*The Ontario Globe*

"Easily the finest biography of a mystery writer since the late John Dickson Carr's superb 1949 life of Conan Doyle.'"—*St. Louis Globe*

"It has taken John McAleer's formidable biography to bring home just how singular and versatile Rex Todhunter Stout was…solid and interesting."—*San Francisco Examiner*

"Do pull down *Rex Stout: A Biography* for a look. It reads like the wind."—*The Evening Sun*, Baltimore

"A fascinating book.Covering the eventful life of this amazing man [Rex Stout], it could hardly be less."—*The News and Observer*, Raleigh.

"…an extremely clever and surprisingly entertaining mystery.Austin Layman is as witty and brilliant as any first-class detective…. [John] McAleer has provided us with more than the run-of-the-mill adventurous risk-takers; these characters have a winning sense of humor."—*St. Louis Post-Dispatch*

"McAleer [has] a dazzling capacity to intellectually amuse and delight.[*Coign of Vantage*] effervesces with urbane wit, and is sprinkled with wryly apt historical and literary references."—*The Buffalo News*

"A worthy effort in every respect… [John McAleer] does his subject justice— Fine research, a clear judicious eye, a keen critical sense, a felicitous style… there's never a dull moment in his perceptive opus."—*Publishers Weekly*

"The definitive account by a master biographer."—Jacques Barzun

"Like father, like son, is, in this case, a very good thing. *Mystery Writing in a Nutshell* combines the best of both McAleers and is first rate."—Robert B. Parker

"*Mystery Writing in a Nutshell* is superbly organized and very highly recommended as being one of the best introductory guides to writing commercially successful mysteries available to aspiring writers and novice writers today."—*Midwest Book Review*

"Simple and straightforward—the nuts and bolts of writing mysteries."—*Kirkus*

"In the minimalist tradition of Walter Mosley's *This Year You Write Your Novel*, you'll find that *Mystery Writing in a Nutshell* packs a lot of punch per page."–American Society of Journalists and Authors

"This is a superb book… All friends of Rex Stout, Nero Wolfe, and Archie Goodwin are in John McAleer's debt."—*Saturday Review of Literature*

"*The 101 Habits of Highly Successful Novelists*…a straightforward, no nonsense, professional approach to fiction writing."—Bill Pronzini

"After all these years, I still learned a few things myself from *Mystery Writing in a Nutshell*. I'm sure you will too."—Edward D. Hoch

"Andrew and John McAleer's *Mystery Writing in a Nutshell* is like brainstorming with a smart and savvy writing pal."—Hank Phillippi Ryan

Synopses

The Big Push and Legend of Sir Morleans' Lost Pearls

When a distinguished London barrister confides in private detective Henry von Stray about the family secrets and legends of a Baroness—revered for her service as a spy on behalf of the Crown during the Great War—von Stray and his trusted companion Professor John Dilpate are forced to leave their comfortable Berkeley Street lodgings and take on what promises to be their most baffling and intriguing case yet.

The Case of the Illustrious Banker

An ingenious adversary has private detective Henry von Stray and his able collaborator in the detection of crime Professor John Dilpate, up against a nippy bit of work when Inspector Renyalds of Scotland Yard enlists them to unravel the puzzling mystery behind the locked-room murder of a notorious bank president.

A Little Birdie Tells Von Stray

When a beautiful young heiress of a high-ranking British official is found brutally murdered in a locked wine cellar, clutching a mysterious dying clue, private detective Henry von Stray and his trusted companion Professor John Dilpate must solve one impossible puzzle after another before they can execute von Stray's brilliant ruse to catch the ruthless killer.

Von Stray and the Five-Fingered Fraudster

A perchance encounter with a Special Agent of His Majesty's Customs Service results in private detective Henry von Stray and his colleague Professor John Dilpate suddenly finding themselves thrust into a race against time as they attempt to thwart the nefarious scheme of a criminal mastermind determined to outfox the Crown.

Publisher's Note

The Amazing History of Private Detective Henry von Stray

London-based detective Henry von Stray's entrance into the world of crime fiction may rank as one of the most fascinating and intriguing developments in the genre's history. Edgar Allan Poe Award winner John McAleer created von Stray in 1937 however, Great Depression duties and McAleer's World War II service interrupted the accounts of von Stray's exciting exploits. A hiatus, incidentally, that would last more than eight decades. According to McAleer's 1937 diary, he wrote at least three von Stray mysteries, yet the only manuscript known to survive the original series is "The Case of the Illustrious Banker," discovered in 2020 by his son Paul, a curator of his father's papers. Its discovery and subsequent publication in *Edgar & Shamus Go Golden* (2022) make von Stray, in all probability, the last of the great master detectives to emerge from the Golden Age of Detective Fiction (a literary period existing predominately during the 1920s and 1930s). With this illustrious moniker in mind, a quest to locate the mysterious disappearance of the remaining manuscripts continues. In the meantime, mystery enthusiasts have waited long enough for the elusive von Stray to share more of his adventures, and now, thanks to McAleer's son Andrew, the long wait is over. In the first ever von Stray collection *A Casebook of Crime*, Andrew, a mystery writer, classic crime fiction educator at Boston College, and U.S. Army Historian, seamlessly picks up where the elder McAleer left off, brilliantly and authentically capturing—and not without a touch of light humor—von Stray's thrilling adventures and unique methods of crime detection through 1920s England. So authentic in fact, mystery lovers will virtually travel back in time to a bygone era where they will genuinely feel as if they're enjoying timeless, never-before-seen century-old classic puzzle whodunits.

Introduction

by Art Taylor

The discovery of hidden papers sounds like something out of a mystery novel or maybe a spy story.

Make those papers a manuscript and have that manuscript hidden for eighty years, and you have yourself the start of an adventure novel.

For the McAleer family, a hidden manuscript was a little of all that: an adventure into the world of mystery. The treasure at adventure's end is the book you're holding in your hand now—and as you'll discover, there's a spy story in the mix too.

And none of it would've happened if a famed professor with a love of the genre hadn't written mystery fiction himself in his much (much!) younger days.

In the mystery world today, John J. McAleer is best known as an Edgar Award-winning nonfiction writer—author of *Rex Stout: A Biography*, published in 1977 and still the definitive study of Stout and his work.

In the academic world, he was the author of books on both Emerson and Thoreau and a much-loved professor of English at Boston College, a teaching career begun in 1948 and spanning a half-century beyond.

And he was a fiction writer himself as well, both of a Korean War novel, *Unit Pride* (1981), and a murder mystery, *Coign of Vantage: The Boston Athenaeum Murders* (1988). As he told the *Boston Globe* the year after that novel's publication, students in his crime writing class "kept asking me what mysteries I'd written, so I thought I'd better produce one."

What he didn't tell those students—what he apparently told no one—was that he'd tried his hand at mysteries long, long before.

At the age of 13, in fact.

"I am writing detective stories," McAleer wrote in his diary on August 4, 1937. "So far I have written three, 'The Case of the Illustrious Banker'; 'The Murder Case at Lord Beachly's'; and the one I am writing now is 'The Case of Sir Morleans' Lost Pearls.' The name of the detective is Henry von Stray."

(In addition to writing detective stories, the young McAleer also had plans to be a detective himself; he announced his new agency in January of that same year, arming his detective kit with a small flashlight, a mirror, a compass, fingerprint powder and brush, a whistle, pencil, fake mustache, knife, ruler, and magnifying glass. Spoiler alert! No flask full of brandy like von Stray now totes in his own investigative bag.)

The first of McAleer's manuscripts from that year, "The Case of the Illustrious Banker," was discovered in his papers eight decades later by his son Paul, and genius detective Henry von Stray and his companion Professor John Dilpate (a narrator in the Watson tradition) finally made their debut in December 2022 in the anthology *Edgar and Shamus Go Golden: Twelve Tales of Murder, Mystery, and Master Detection.*

Another of McAleer's sons, Andrew, co-edited that volume with Gay Toltl Kinman, and the elder McAleer's story provided both the occasion and the indirect inspiration for the entire volume, which invited Edgar and Shamus Award-winning authors to pen their own tales inspired—as McAleer was—by the traditions of the Golden Age of Mystery.

In a press release celebrating the anthology, Paul drew on the diary entry and promised, "You can bet a quest to locate more von Stray stories is afoot!"

But what if those stories couldn't be found?

Enter Andrew McAleer again, slipping off his editor's hat and sitting down at the keyboard in a fresh way.

Like his father, Andrew is a novelist who has taught crime fiction at Boston College, and father and son had already collaborated on a book previously: *Mystery Writing in a Nutshell: The World's Most Concise Guide to Mystery and Suspense Writing*, praised by *Kirkus* as "brief, well-outlined guide for budding mystery writers."

If the elder McAleer's lost pearls were indeed lost in another way, the younger one would write a story himself around that idea—following von Stray and Dilpate into a new adventure, channeling his father's style, tone, and humor, diving back into 1920s England and the world of the Golden Age detective story, and building further on the world that his father had constructed in that era—a world that had nearly been lost.

Recovering that first story was a brilliant find, but continuing the series reveals a different kind of brilliance. More than mimicry or some elevated form of pastiche, these stories—one by John McAleer, three now by Andrew—strike me as true collaborations, the father as a young boy and son as a grown man speaking with one shining voice. Andrew has the benefit of hindsight on the era, and the lead story here "The Big Push and Legend of Sir Morelans' Lost Pearls"—building on the earlier title of "The Case of Sir Moreleans' Lost Pearls"—looks back on the Great War for a story that combines the mystery and the spy story and a bit of family drama in exciting ways. Another of John McAleer's titles, "The Murder Case at Lord Beachly's," (re-titled "A Little Birdie Tells Von Stray") has inspired an impossible puzzle story about the murder of a young heiress, her body found in a locked wine cellar. A final story, "Von Stray and the Five-Fingered Fraudster," draws on a striking conceit—a shipment of gloves, left-handed only! —for a tale that once again showcases von Stray's cleverness, and with the bonus of being set aboard a train, a classic Golden Age setting.

Gathering these stories together, *A Casebook of Crime* showcases a son honoring his father's legacy with generosity and grace. It's commemoration and continuation both—and a fine gift for us readers too.

Here's hoping for even more mysterious adventures ahead indeed!

I

The Big Push

Andrew McAleer

*From the Desk of
Professor John W. Dilpate
Berkeley Square, London
7 July 1923*

I: Sir Hamilton Wade Huddersfield, KC

Of all the mysterious adventures I have had the honor to serve as the great private detective Henry von Stray's closest confidant and trusted assistant, few have reached the same intriguing and exciting dimensions as the baffling case concerning The Big Push and Legend of Sir Morleans' Lost Pearls.

The mysterious affair began on the beautiful spring morning of May the eighth in the year 1923. I was on a rare sabbatical from the University Clifford and spent the morning in my study located in the lodgings I share with von Stray at 121B Berkeley Street, London. I was engaged in some rather difficult research regarding the classification of an extinct South American beetle and making significant progress when a ringing doorbell interrupted my work.

Upon opening the door, I couldn't have been more astounded. Before me stood the lean figure of a distinguished looking gentleman, appearing not quite sixty, whom I recognized immediately as London's preeminent barrister Sir Hamilton Wade Huddersfield, KC. His reputation as a trial attorney and *pro bono* advocate for the men returning from the War was second to none. I could not for the life of me imagine why he would be calling at our doorstep; but would soon learn he wished to engage von Stray on behalf of the bravest and most elusive heroines of the War.

"Good morning, Professor Dilpate," he said in a crisp baritone while removing his top hat and following it with a slight, dignified nod.

I was flabbergasted this distinguished member of the bar—a King's Counsel no less—knew my name.

I quickly surmised Sir Hamilton must have taken notice of my puzzlement in his recognizing me. He continued his amiable greeting. "I am in the presence of Mr. Henry von Stray's coadjutor, Professor John W. Dilpate am I not?"

"Indeed, sir. Indeed. My sincerest apologies, I wasn't aware you knew of me."

"I have the honor of serving as a University Clifford trustee and have sedulously followed your fascinating scientific work on behalf of the University. Your recent scholarly works in the *Journal of Entomology* cross-indexing the nocturnal eating habits of leaf beetles has not escaped my notice."

"Thank you, sir. I think you will find my latest discoveries with respect to the Eumolpinae will add further prestige to Clifford. They are, as I am sure you are quite familiar, a subfamily of leaf beetles and I am presently on the verge—"

Sir Hamilton interrupted me in a judicious manner. "I am most interested to learn more about your erudite discoveries, Professor, nevertheless, I must speak with Mr. von Stray on an urgent matter."

"Indeed, sir. You are most welcome. Please come inside. I will arrange for von Stray to meet with you at once, in the sitting room upstairs. I know he would be quite honored to offer whatever assistance he can."

After escorting our guest into the sitting room and seating him into my easy chair overlooking Berkeley Street, I located von Stray in the kitchen. He was busy jarring a batch of his superb homemade Yorkshire rhubarb jam. Von Stray became an excellent cook after his service in the trenches during the War. The intoxicating aroma of the rhubarb and his own secret blends of spices and honey made me forget momentarily about Sir Hamilton's pressing matter. I soon rallied, however.

"I must interrupt, von Stray!" I cleared my throat. "Sir Hamilton Wade Huddersfield is here to consult you on what he has entrusted me to inform you is an urgent matter."

Von Stray ladled the steaming mixture into a mason jar. "What could be more urgent than jarring my scrumptious Yorkshire rhubarb? I have everything at the precise temperature and if I don't jar the mixture now, we'll be lathering our Scottish oatcakes with coagulated lumps of pectin for the foreseeable future."

"Von Stray you can't be serious!"

"Only two more jars to go, Professor. See if you can occupy our distinguished, but unexpected guest."

In the sitting room I did my best to entertain Sir Hamilton. "My apologies, Sir Hamilton, von Stray will be out momentarily. Perhaps I could show you my study where I conduct my beetle experiments and classifications? I'm presently classifying an extinct South American specimen. What I find most astonishing about this rather mercurial beetle is…"

Just as I began my fascinating lecture von Stray swept into the sitting room, his London briar pipe in hand. "Thank you for waiting, Sir Hamilton and please excuse my delay," von Stray said in his customary thoughtful tone. "My colleague advises me you are here on an urgent matter?"

Sir Hamilton rubbed his hands together. "Indeed. I am here at the request of a client who must be assured of your full discretion."

I sat in von Stray's easy chair as my companion leaned against the fireplace mantle. Von Stray then reached into the right-side pocket of his blazer for his pipe tobacco pouch and filled his pipe with deliberate care. "You can always count on my discretion, and I assure you Professor Dilpate's as well. There is no one I trust more."

I was astounded. Sir Hamilton, one of our greatest orators, struggled to find the words to describe whatever difficulty plagued this mysterious client of his. "My sincerest apologies, von Stray. Yours and the Professor's discretion concerning such matters is well known and need not be subjected to oath."

Von Stray gently rubbed the scar located on the upper left side of his forehead. He calls this scar his 'memento' from his days in the trenches during the War, and has a tendency to rub it while in deep thought. "Please, no need to apologize, Sir Hamilton. You have every right and even a duty to protect your client's interests and sensitive matters."

"Thank you, von Stray." Our guest coughed into a silk handkerchief before disclosing the object of his visit. "I have been asked to pay you this visit on behalf of Lady Elizabeth Victoria Thornbred."

I raised my gold-rimmed spectacles. "Good heavens!"

Her Ladyship came from one of the finest families in England and although she hailed from a background cloaked in silk and society, her espionage exploits as a secret agent on behalf of the Crown and its allies during the War were invaluable. Her legendary clandestine accounts under the code name "Ariadne" tell of secreting into Germany where, with the aid of her American counterpart—even to this day his identity remains a secret and is known only to the public by his code name "Theseus"—she ran a dogged underground counter-espionage campaign to disseminate misinformation about false allied troop movements and bogus Royal Navy blockade strategies. Nary was there a time when she did not somehow manage to smuggle out of the hands of the Kaiser and into the hands of His Majesty, the blueprints for Germany's latest weaponry scheme. It also has been said that Lady Elizabeth caught the Kaiser flatfooted when she convinced him that the Americas would never join the war effort. When her daring exploits became known after the War—as part of the Parliament's campaign to boost the peoples' morale by showing everyone from cabbage to king had done their part—there wasn't a soldier or sailor who didn't believe his survival from the trenches or blockade was, in some measure, spared due to the dangerous and courageous assignments carried out by this indefatigable woman. Von Stray, and myself included.

After a heavy silence von Stray said, "Please, Sir Hamilton, tell us how we can be of service to her Ladyship."

Sir Hamilton rose slowly from his seat, turned his back to us and stared out at Berkeley Street as he spoke. "For that von Stray, we must visit an area of family legend, secrets, and intrigue. I cannot vouch for truth, accuracy, or veracity to any of what I am about to share." He turned away from the window and faced us. "Nevertheless, I can state with certainty that Lady Elizabeth takes the firm position that your knowledge of this background is vital for your assistance and guidance in ensuring that her estate, Suckling Manor, is passed to her rightful heir without encumbrance."

Von Stray lit his pipe and then said thoughtfully, "Pray tell, who is her rightful heir?"

"Her Ladyship's nephew Sir Ambrose Nelson Morleans," he replied, returning to his seat. "As you may be aware, Her Ladyship's husband Colonel James Hobson Thornbred was killed during the Boer War. Sir Ambrose's father, Lieutenant Colonel George Nelson Morleans, served under Thornbred's command. He also perished in the same useless skirmish with a Boer guerilla unit. By all accounts, Sir Ambrose's mother died of a broken heart shortly after hearing the shocking news of her husband. Naturally, Lady Elizabeth, who was without child, raised Sir Ambrose as if he were her own son. She loves Sir Ambrose dearly and will take any measure in order to ensure his rightful legacy passes to him."

I said, "I daresay death taxes alone will make that a formidable task with the Crown scooping upwards of fifty percent of these old estates."

There was the slightest hesitation before our guest responded. "Eh… perhaps, Professor…however that is an issue for my office to handle at a later time."

Von Stray moved us off the ugly topic of death taxes. "Hopefully for Lady Elizabeth's sake and England's at a *much* later time. In any event, I must confess to having heard unflattering rumblings of Sir Ambrose being a rather high-spirited young man who has been having difficulty adjusting after the War. Nevertheless, knowing of his bloodline, I refuse to credit these pernicious rumors. I mention this because I fear your visit has some connection with this scandalous scuttlebutt."

I had come to the same conclusion as von Stray and joined him in urging our guest to tell us how we could help her Ladyship. "Please, sir, you may continue in complete confidence."

Sir Hamilton heaved a profound sigh. He said, his voice somber, "I regret to inform you there is a kernel of truth in the rumors, gentlemen. I'm sure you have both heard of the horrific fate of Morleans' Mates during the big push— the Battle of the Somme to be specific, but what I am about to share with you is Sir Ambrose's fate during the doomed battle. To begin, like so many young men—boys really—when he heard of Lord Kitchener's alluring promise: 'If you joined together, you served together.' Sir Ambrose was caught up in the surge of patriotism sweeping through the nation. His classmates shared the same enthusiasm. In their excitement to answer the Crown's call they formed a volunteer regiment naming it, Morleans' Mates. They were going to rid the world of bullies and tyrants. As they paraded off to war past the cheering crowds, they were still wearing their Sunday finery."

Von Stray glanced up at the portrait of his great-grandfather Captain Frederick von Stray hanging above the sitting room's fireplace. Captain von Stray served as a distinguished Danish infantry officer in the previous century and my companion holds this man whom he never met in the highest regard. He said, in a tone reminiscent of a confessional whisper, "I can remember the same patriotic sentiment surging through my veins." My colleague looked at me and nodded. "As does the Professor."

"Yes," I said, agreeing with von Stray. "I can still see the recruitment slogans: 'Women of Britain Say Go!' and 'Your Country Needs You!' Whether it was passion or guilt, most young men soon found themselves in the clutches of a military recruiter."

Von Stray said, after what seemed like a long period of reflection, "None of us could foresee the dark days of mud and blood ahead while holding the line. Pray continue, sir."

"Prior to the charge on the Somme," Sir Hamilton said, "the British engaged in a massive artillery bombardment that promised to wipe out the Germans. You gentlemen need little reminding of the disaster that followed—the bombardment strategy failed miserably."

Von Stray, who had somehow managed to survive the battle, winced slightly. "Respectfully, sir, that depends on one's perspective. The bombardment failed miserably for our side—not Germany's."

"Quite true, von Stray. It turned out to be little more than a dust bath to the well-fortified German trench system. When the bombardment ended, whistles announcing the attack blew. Ambrose clambered over the top of his trench to make the charge, but as soon as he and his mates surfaced, a German artillery barrage rained down on the whole British line with frightening accuracy. Ambrose never made it past No Man's Land. A shell hit the trench and a chunk of wood from one of the railway sleepers used as a trench support knocked him unconscious. He was out of the fight. The

Mates, like so many other regiments, were massacred. He continues to blame himself for not being there with them when they perished. Her Ladyship has even sought help from this latest form of treatment known as 'psychology.' Unfortunately, the results have been limited."

I have always had my doubts about this new form of treatment. Intellectual stimulation rounded off with arduous toil, such as my daily Indian club exercise regimen, has always been the best way to bolster one's outlook. I said firmly, "The lad must understand he did his duty and then some. That's all anyone can expect. He must simply put the incident behind him and forget the War. It's a miracle anyone survived the mayhem and carnage, but the ones who did must continue to put their best foot forward."

Von Stray bit down on the tip of his pipe. "We must never forget the trenches, Professor, anymore than forget your brave service in the Naval blockade."

I was insistent. "I agree, von Stray; I'm merely saying the man did his duty and that he must buck up and not blame himself for surviving. It's that simple."

My colleague pulled me back on track. "Perhaps we should table this discussion for another day. We must give Sir Hamilton our fullest attention and learn how we can serve Lady Elizabeth."

Seeing the wisdom of my friend's position, I gave Sir Hamilton my undivided attention as he confided in us the remarkable history and secrets of one of England's most notable families.

II: Lord George Eustace Morleans

"Regarding our present dilemma," Sir Hamilton took a deep breath, "I will begin with Lady Elizabeth's great grandfather George Eustace Morleans, for he is the one who first brought prestige and title to the family. Sir Morleans was originally an idler fortune seeker. As the son of a Ramsgate fisherman, he was expected to follow in his father's trade as all the male line had done for generations. Young George had other plans, however. While still in his teens he stowed away from England in a merchant vessel to the West Indies where he failed at every venture and scheme he endeavored to pursue. In financial debt and ruin, he managed to escape his creditors and ultimately ended up in the Orient where he succeeded in duplicating his failures from the West Indies. With creditors once again at his heels, out of desperation to escape, he joined an expedition of the Artic seas. During this latest adventure he discovered and honed his skills as a master seaman. His adventures in the Artic seas completed, he made his way to San Jaun del Norte where he became a highly regarded sea merchant and eventually paid off all his debts with interest."

"By Jove!" I said, "who would have suspected Sir Morleans came from such humble stock."

Our guest elevated his eyebrows. "Some day, Professor, I shall share with you my ancestors' humble origins." He then ventured on with his account of the facts as he knew them. "Just as things could not have looked more prosperous for the young Morleans, he developed a fever that invalided him, and forced him to return to England where he convalesced for some eighteen months. Thankfully, he made a miraculous recovery and when he did, a patriotic fire stoked within him. He described this fervor to friends as a "hot shot" burning inside him. As it turns out, his love of England could not have coupled fate at a more opportune time. When war broke out with revolutionary France, he enlisted in the Royal Navy where his superiors soon recognized his superior skills as a master seaman. As a result, he found himself under the direct command of none other than Horatio Nelson. Morleans was with Nelson when he pursued a great French armament under the command of Napoleon, who was then determined to conquer Egypt. With Morleans aiding him in no small measure, Nelson tracked Napoleon down, ultimately leading to the Battle of the Nile on August 1st 1798. Moreleans so distinguished himself during the battle that Nelson privately credited him with having profound influence over the victory."

"An important day for England that cannot be understated," von Stray added.

"You know your history, von Stray," Sir Hamilton complimented. "The victory in the Nile proved to be one of the most important in England's naval history as it returned England's prestige in the Mediterranean. Morleans became one of Nelson's own as it were and was made a baronet after a few whispers from Lord Nelson in the appropriate circles."

Von Stray drew thoughtfully on his pipe. Notes of cocoa and molasses aroma drifted through the room. "Respectfully, Sir Hamilton, I am most interested to learn how this familial history will serve us in resolving Lady Elizabeth's current predicament—the specifics of which you are yet to divulge."

"You have been most patient, gentlemen, but this familial history is necessary if I am to impress upon you the significance of a family heirloom passed down from Sir Morleans and ultimately to Lady Elizabeth. You have heard of the Morleans pearls and the legend of their provenance?"

"Indeed," I said. "They are considered by many respected experts to be the finest set of matched pearls in the world. Lord Nelson himself presented them to Sir Morleans if I am not mistaken."

"You are not, Professor," Sir Hamilton affirmed. "It is my unfortunate duty to advise you that they have been reported…missing."

"Great Scott!" I exclaimed; unable to control my shock. "My apologies, Sir Hamilton for my outburst."

Our visitor kindly overlooked my excited utterance. "It's quite all right, Professor. Your genuine concern for Lady Elizabeth is most appreciated. I'm afraid she has experienced quite a shock over the events. She wishes to engage you to solve the mystery behind their strange disappearance. Moreover, time is of the essence. Her Ladyship is convinced that the pearls must be found before the petals fall off Suckling Manor's prized magnolia tree. Sir Morleans planted the tree, and no other ornamental tree pays a finer tribute to Suckling."

Von Stray's eyebrows were drawn together tightly as he paced the room in intense thought. "I find it rather interesting that her Ladyship has formed some nexus between the missing pearls and the life expectancy of the magnolia's flowers. Although I have never met her, she does not strike me as someone who forms arbitrary and capricious theories. Could it be that she connects the life expectancy of the petals with her own?"

Sir Hamilton looked forlorn. "I have come to the same dreadful conclusion, von Stray. Her Ladyship's reasoning is without scientific basis. Regardless, there is no convincing her otherwise. She insists that the pearls must be located before the petals drop. Otherwise, she will be unable to pass Suckling Manor to Sir Ambrose."

"Quite intriguing," said von Stray, as he studied our guest, who was currently in the process of adjusting his seating position. "What of the pearls themselves? Refresh my recollection of their legend?"

"The pearls are of a Chinese origin. As you likely know, the Chinese pearl culture is carried to the greatest of perfection. In fact, they have been able to make their own pearls for thousands of years. Documents dating back as early as a 1000 B.C. tell how a Chinese native of Hoochow named, Ye-Jin-Yang, developed a process for making pearls by using a small, forked bamboo stick to insert bits of bone into the valves of river-mussels. In a few months, the mussels would form a pearl around the bone. Family legend is that Sir Morleans pearls were made in such a way using bone fragments from none other than Julius Caesar."

I was agog. "Most fascinating."

"Yes. I recall the legend now," said von Stray. "This remarkable tale claims that the magnificent pink hue adorning the pearls is the blood and spirit of Caesar himself."

I waved a hand dubiously at my companion. "A fantastic fairytale, old man." It was all I could do from saying "Great Caesar's ghost!"

Von Stray whisked his pipe stem in my direction and nodded. "Tale indeed, Dilpate, and while highly improbable, it doesn't alter the fact that the pearls seem to have a stronghold over their owners as coveted objects have a tendency to do rather than the other way around."

Sir Hamilton rubbed his chin. "I think you have hit upon the crux of the case, von Stray."

"Pray, Sir Hamilton, do you know of any conceivable reason why Her Ladyship believes the pearls' disappearance determine the fate of Suckling Manor?"

"She is quite right, von Stray. On this point I can provide you with legal specifics. The family trust contains a caveat that Suckling Manor can be conveyed only to a rightful heir in possession of the pearls. The monetary value of the pearls was subordinate to Sir Morleans. As you stated earlier, he claimed Lord Nelson gifted him the pearls and shared with him their legend. To Sir Morleans, the pearls represented the very foundation of Suckling Manor and his surname."

As a coleopterist, my scientific studies of beetles often lead to the examination of plant life. This knowledge proved invaluable to the investigation. "Magnolia flowers have the approximate life expectancy of a fortnight."

"Thank you, Professor," von Stray said, before addressing our guest. "Tell me, Sir Hamilton, when did Lady Elizabeth first notice of the pearls' disappearance?"

"Wednesday morning."

Von Stray continued. "Yesterday. And when did the magnolia's flowers blossom?"

"According to Her Ladyship's senior footman Norman Massey, this past Sunday saw the magnolia in full bloom."

Von Stray quickly knocked out his pipe into the fireplace. "Make short work of packing your kit, Dilpate. Your fortnight has dwindled to ten days!"

III: The Passenger Train to Ramsgate

I was packed in two shakes of a lamb's tail taking only the most essential items for our unexpected journey to Suckling Manor. I scarcely had time to stow my moustache grooming kit and Indian exercising clubs; essential instruments for my daily workout regimen.

As I dashed into the sitting room, von Stray had his Gladstone bag and his battered leather bag full of investigative instruments gripped in one hand and, with his other hand, flipped on his ancient, but trusty wool-tweed cap. As we made for the stairs, I pulled my light-blue linen newsboy cap off its respective peg and was on Berkeley Street in less time than it takes to tell.

With great effort we managed to catch the next southeastern passenger train from London, to the Ramsgate Harbor Station. In the privacy of our first-class passenger compartment, we discussed the trust's strange caveat concerning the pearls.

"Tell me, Sir Hamilton," von Stray began, "in your legal opinion, is the caveat enforceable? Considering that such an item could easily be lost or stolen, as is presently the case, it seems rather draconian that the fate of Suckling rests solely in their possession from generation to generation."

"Quite right, von Stray. That is my legal opinion. I doubt a court would uphold the restriction. Notwithstanding, one can never guarantee what a court is inclined to do. There are at least two points to consider. Firstly, Lady Elizabeth insists on its relevancy. There is no persuading her otherwise. Secondly, there is a distant relative lurking in the wings waiting to find some pretext to upturn the estate. If the pearls are missing, he would have viable grounds—no matter how remote—to challenge Sir Ambrose's rightful possession should Lady Elizabeth pass to her reward prior to the pearls' return. A nuisance case of this kind could go on for years and I fear Sir Ambrose is not presently up to the legal challenge."

"I see," said von Stray. "The result would be much the same as if the caveat were upheld by a court. Sir Ambrose would be forced to settle the claim with this distant, but now interested relative's legal challenge and hence, Suckling Manor would be fragmented."

"Precisely. The expense of a legal challenge and the exorbitant death duties introduced after the War would leave, at best, a mere pittance remaining for Ambrose."

I asked, "Who is this cousin?"

"Mr. Edward Smethwick of Leeds. He is on holiday at Suckling now and is well aware of the dilemma."

Von Stray lit his pipe. "What do you know of Mr. Smethwick?"

Sir Hamilton shook his head. "He purports to be a businessman of some sort. Until now, I've had no real cause to investigate him."

"Perhaps," von Stray suggested, "when we reach Ramsgate, your office could make the necessary enquiries."

"Excellent idea, von Stray. I have offices in Ramsgate and will attend to it immediately."

I have to confess I saw no purpose in digging into Smethwick. On this score, von Stray was unquestionably on the wrong trail. The pearls were lost and considering how time was of the essence, our efforts would be better spent finding them. Once we located them—I felt confident we would—immediate issues regarding the estate would cease. As a result, cousin Smethwick would be out of luck. For the moment, however, what to do about the mysterious Smethwick was settled. Accordingly, I brought up an immediate pressing concern—lunch.

With some skillful prodding on my end, we decided to take an early lunch in the dining carriage. There we enjoyed a most wonderful arrangement of oyster patties, deviled kidneys, and some delicious raspberry and goat cheese clamshell cakes. A few other passengers also took lunch in the dining carriage including a strange Bohemian-looking man wearing a rumpled grey flannel suit. A heavy black beard concealed his face and between bites of his egg salad sandwich, he whispered to himself while reading Shakespeare's *The Tempest*. We couldn't help but notice the man, however, since he had nothing whatsoever to do with the case, I spent the rest of our journey enjoying the sweeping view of the English countryside.

After alighting the train at Ramsgate, Sir Hamilton informed us he would take immediate charge of the Smethwick issue. Before bidding us a rather hasty farewell, he advised us he could be reached through his head secretary of his London office.

When Sir Hamilton was out of earshot von Stray consulted with me, as he often does, on the more complicated areas of a case. "Tell me, Dilpate," he said, pausing for a brief moment to glance over his left shoulder toward the end of the platform, "considering how Sir Hamilton fears a nuisance lawsuit from Smethwick could dissolve the Morleans estate and leave Sir Ambrose all but destitute, does his claim to know so little of cousin Smethwick strike you as peculiar?"

I readily agreed with my colleague. "Quite so, von Stray. I immediately came to the same conclusion—yet had been reluctant to question Sir Hamilton on this point." Just as I had finished speaking, I looked over von Stray's left shoulder in time to observe the man with the heavy black beard climb onto a shiny Rudge-Whitworth push-bicycle and pedal away.

I smiled. "Look, von Stray, our strange friend from the dining carriage. I wonder what sort of dealings a man such as he could be engaged."

"Yes, Dilpate," von Stray said, rubbing his scar, "I have been pondering the same question."

IV: Suckling Manor

fter a rough, and tumble hansom ride over unspoiled country lanes winding from the railway station to Suckling Manor, our approximately three-hour journey from the comfortable surroundings of our London flat concluded. Suckling is located in a secluded, beautifully manicured enclave of Ramsgate known as Gurnet Village. On a map it appears as little more than a finger of land poking around the Strait of Dover, yet a whole way of life exists here. The seascape village hangs on by its eyebrows on the South-Eastern edge of England and at its most extreme eastern point—the tip of Gurnet's finger—stands its magnificent lighthouse on a tiny bluff jutting out into the ocean in defiance of Poseidon.

Gurnet is everything the outsider might imagine: a simple unspoiled fishing and farming hamlet consisting of little more than a wooden dock extending into its harbor, a dozen shops, publick house, sprinkling of ancient cottages dotting the countryside, twisting sand-stone lanes, and a weather-beaten flint-faced church. This secluded patch of England appears to be the quintessential village untouched by the ever-twitching hands of Father Time. Nevertheless, quaint architecture, cramped English gardens, and rejuvenating sea-breezes belie its tragic history.

Like many English villages, Gurnet was primarily unknown to outsiders until the War when it became an indelible symbol of what can happen when a petty aristocrat, such as the Kaiser, unleashes a combustible mixture consisting of modern weaponry and idle grudges. For far too many, Gurnet brought the realities of the war to the home-front when the horrific news of the massacre of Morleans' Mates reached our shores. A generation of young men lost to the vengeful whims of bullheaded officers who armed their soldiers with little more than promises and foolproof battle plans destined to fail well before execution.

As we stepped out of the hansom, and onto Suckling's cobblestone forecourt, I took a moment to consume the fresh sea air and admire the estate's view. The hulking Manor House of Suckling stood high on a cliff overlooking the Strait of Dover. It was breathtaking. The 16th-century Manor House constructed of tens of thousands of sea-stones fitted by men who passed to their reward hundreds of years ago looked as structurally sound as if the stones had been rested on pads of mortar yesterday. The lush-green ivy hugging the foundation at a height of about fifteen feet complemented the stones beautifully as did the meticulously groomed English gardens, rolling hills of clipped sod, and bridle pathways. From the forecourt, a seemingly endless ribbon of crushed-clamshell driveway divided the estate's front grounds. Background to all of this manmade beauty, a relentless ocean could be heard as it pounded the cliff towering over the beachhead—a grim reminder that someday the sea would reclaim what man had taken.

As we faced the hulking sea-stone Manor House, von Stray said, pointing easterly, "Look to your left, Dilpate. This beautiful magnolia is undoubtedly the tree in question." He pointed to a magnificent magnolia blooming in a glorious pinkish blaze. "Note its great height extending as high as the first floor, its close proximity to the house, and how it's located on the eastern side facing the ocean."

Not wanting to embarrass my friend, I hid my smile concerning his lack of knowledge regarding the scientific study of plants. "I wouldn't count your preliminary observations as clues yet, von Stray. The tree's location I can state without question has no bearing on this case whatsoever. I'm quite certain it was planted on the eastern side simply to take advantage of the morning sun. As far as its height and close proximity to the structure, I can again state without hesitation that a lack of proper pruning and balancing of the tree is the prime culprit."

Von Stray complimented me profusely on my logical analysis. "Thank you,

Professor. I must keep your botanical observations foremost in my thoughts when forming my final conclusions in this intriguing case."

No sooner had my companion uttered his complement when we found ourselves turning around suddenly at the sound of clamshells crackling under feet came from behind. A gentleman of approximately fifty stood before us. He had a healthy, ruddy complexion undoubtedly borne from regimented living and hearty English fare. He wore a long-tailed black jacket over his soldierly physique and a Royal Welsh Fusiliers collar badge from the Boer war hung on the jacket's lapel. He clicked his heels while introducing himself. "Good afternoon, gentlemen. I'm her Ladyship's senior footman Norman Massey. Sir Hamilton advised me you would be arriving. Please accept my apologies for not greeting you, but I had some important business to attend to with the head gardener, Theodore."

Von Stray touched the brim of his cap. "No apologies necessary, sir. We have been admiring your exceptional work in maintaining the estate. I am Henry von Stray, and this is my colleague, Professor John Dilpate."

Massey's smile appeared to combine concern with relief. "Thank you, sir. I am quite familiar with your superior exploits as a criminologist. You and Professor Dilpate are most kind to assist her Ladyship."

I said to our new friend, "As veterans of the War, we are undoubtedly in Lady Elizabeth's debt."

Massey nodded. "You are most kind, Professor."

"We were admiring your magnificent magnolia tree," von Stray suddenly announced with great enthusiasm. "I can see why Sir Hamilton informed us it's the estate's centerpiece."

"Indeed, sir."

"Yes," I added. "However, I hope your discussion with the head gardener included instructions to prune and balance the tree. After its blossoms have fallen of course."

Massey paused for a moment before forming his response. "I assure you, Professor the necessary pruning will occur *after* the blossoms fall."

V: Shellshock

Massey escorted us into the home's foyer where we were greeted by a disheveled man who didn't appear quite yet thirty. He cut a strapping athletic pose yet seemed oblivious that his golfing attire of beige knickers, red and green patterned socks, matching sweater vest and soft cap was powdered with heavy dust and random bits of hay stem.

"Blimey! Well, well. Hallo!" the greeter mocked as he slid his fingers along my lapel. "If it isn't the boys of the volunteer regiment here to rescue her nibs. You're too late—gentlemen. Can't save them now. They've all gone over the hill quite some time ago to the four winds of heaven. All scuttled off like a busted string of *pearls* bouncing off into the parade lane only to get squashed. Tootles, boys! Tootles!" His rant complete, the man hurriedly wedged between us and exited through the front door not bothering to shut it behind him.

A forlorn look came over Massey as he gripped his lapels. "Pray, gentlemen, you'll have to excuse himself. He's presently distracted with his inspection of the old stable. No horses since the War, you understand."

In addition to horses being conscripted for use in the War, the exorbitant postwar tax increases have left many a stable empty and many an estate sold at auction.

Von Stray said, "We understand completely, Massey. I take it we have just had the pleasure of meeting Her Ladyship's nephew Sir Ambrose?"

Massey's head bowed slightly. "Indeed, sir."

Sir Hamilton couldn't have prepared me for the shock I received in learning that the great Morleans bloodline hung in the balance of this young man. Lost pearls and estate matters seemed the least of this great family's concerns.

A deep voice fitting a stage actor suddenly consumed the front foyer. "Presently distracted! Sir Ambrose has had half a dozen years to snap out of his *present* condition. He's got himself another case of the jim-jams if you ask me. Out all hours of the night carousing with other slackers. All this coddling nonsense about shell-shock. What he needs is steady work. Roll up the old sleeves, what? The boy's a world-champion idler."

Outside, the rumble of a motorcar sounded and before Massey shut the front door, I could see hunks of clamshell spraying out from under the contraption's back tires as it roared down the long sweep leading away from the estate.

Massey remained dignified. "Gentlemen, allow me the honor of introducing to you Sir Ambrose's second cousin, Mr. Edward Smethwick of Leeds."

Smethwick appeared every bit the business type. A man dancing near sixty he stood about six feet tall and consisted of little more than stern features, polished pince-nez, knife-creased trousers, and hardened collar. The sort of gent who undoubtedly credited himself as a regular John Bull Englishman.

"First cousin once removed!" Smethwick corrected harshly, as he leaned leftward into his ivory-handled walking stick. "You always do that, Massey. Get it right. Shape up or ship out, old man."

Von Stray ignored Smethwick's upbraiding of the senior footman. "Good afternoon, Mr. Smethwick. I am Henry von Stray, and this is my assistant, Professor John Dilpate."

Smethwick whisked off his pince-nez and ejaculated with snorts of superiority, "Good heavens, *man*! Assistant to *what*?"

"I am a private detective. We have been engaged by Lady Elizabeth's attorney Sir Hamilton Wade Huddersfield to help locate the Sir Morleans pearls. You are aware, no doubt, of the claims they have disappeared?"

A burst of scoffs blew out of Smethwick's stentorian pipes. "Fiddle faddle! Missing pearls. Stolen pearls more likely. How do you think my shell-shocked squashy cousin underwrites his nightly haunts?"

Von Stray ventured on. "I take it, Mr. Smethwick you've formed the opinion that Sir Ambrose has something to do with the pearls' disappearance?"

"What kind of private detective are you…?" he sneered. "It's as obvious as an intoxicated mermaid with credit issues whistling 'Ain't We Got Fun' on a toadstool. The boy refuses steady work and lives well beyond his allowance. Less backbone than a shilling's worth of custard."

The great detective politely dismissed Smethwick's scathing attack. "Thank you, Mr. Smethwick. I must keep your observations foremost in my thoughts when forming my final conclusions in this case."

Smethwick flipped on his hounds-tooth walking cap and said, "Yes. Well… good. Keep it in mind. Save my dear precious cousin a lot of time, money, and false hopes. I'm off for a bit of this fresh sea air. If more men filled their lungs with Mother Earth rather than acrid pub odor we'd have fewer problems in this world. I'll see you gentlemen at tea?"

I had forgotten how famished I was. The oyster patties and deviled kidneys seemed like centuries ago. I nodded, "We would be delighted, thank you."

My companion was all business. "So long as it does not conflict with Her Ladyship's instructions."

Smethwick studied von Stray before answering. "Right, Her Ladyship's instructions. How silly of me to forget that my *dear* cousin would have instructions." As Smethwick made for the door, he relied heavily on his walking stick.

Von Stray stopped him. "Enjoy your fresh air, Mr. Smethwick and I hope your handsome walking stick is soon an ornament rather than a means of support."

Smethwick grumbled as he tapped his left foot with the tip of his cane. He was wearing a pair of worn, yet spit-polished pair of Edwardian brogues. "Not hardly. This limp is a permanent gift from the Kaiser himself."

As Smethwick tapped his left foot, von Stray gently massaged his forehead scar. It was here I noticed the gold band around Smethwick's stick separating its ivory handle from its mahogany shaft. Since Smethwick's shoes revealed nothing remarkable, I had no doubt that this gold band is what drew von Stray's attention.

VI: Lady Elizabeth Victoria Thornbred

As Massey led us up to our quarters on the first floor, I took note of the home's interior. It contained the usual objects of parade: Persian rugs, medieval tapestries, gilt-framed portraits, elaborate frescoes, Italian-marble floors arranged in complicated geometric patterns, and rooms trimmed in dark-stained quarter-sawn oak. Spirited deep within the home's venerable walls lived that ancient smell of mysterious bygone eras, which tend to invite echoes of long-forgotten celebrations, life-long secrets, and important victories once coveted by the long departed.

After stowing our gear in our billet, Massey led us down the hallway to Lady Elizabeth's bedroom. "Until Lady Elizabeth recovers," he felt the need to explain before entering, "her bedroom also functions as her study. She insists on maintaining a few correspondences."

After Massey announced us to Her Ladyship, we exchanged a few broadsides of civility, and he dismissed himself.

As we entered the bedroom, its door screeched loudly. I was stunned when I saw this great woman's condition. Her emaciated face wore a waxy-green pallor, and you could count the bones of her hands. A laced night bonnet covered whatever remained of her famous shock of gorgeous red hair. It thwarted my spirits terribly to learn she spent this beautiful spring day bedbound under a light-pink eiderdown while propped up with pillows. I simply couldn't accept that this heroine of the War would spend her remaining days confined to bed.

A handful of years earlier during the War, unsubstantiated rumors of a mysterious, unidentified female English spy's derring-do were legendary and never failed to boost troop morale. Now it seemed the only morale she got in return for her selfless service came from the set of open bay windows to the right of her bed, which rewarded her with a brilliant vista of the magnolia tree and pleasant chirrup notes from the house sparrows visiting the tree and house ivy.

Despite her confined station she greeted us with bushels of English pluck. "This is indeed an honor, gentlemen. Thank you for taking the time to listen to a dying woman's drivel about estate matters. I'm sure you have better things to do. As do you, Catherine!" Lady Elizabeth suddenly changed course and addressed her housemaid, Catherine, who was busy polishing a brass bellpush. She was an unusually beautiful young blond-haired, blue-eyed woman who looked to hold down the good side of twenty-five.

With a graceful carriage Catherine bobbed a slight curtsy and said, "Yes, milady." She then paused for a moment and her eyes shifted and swiveled like a novice stage actress struggling to retrieve her next line. "Er…ahmm…would you like me to empty the…er…dustbin before I go, milady?" She pointed to the dustbin next to a chesterfield sofa.

"Empty the dustbin? You haven't emptied the dustbin in weeks for the simple reason that in my condition I have been unable to make any rubbish to empty! Now scoot. You have plenty to do other than dote over me. I'm sure my guests will quickly grow tiresome of my company and expect tea."

With another curtsy, Catherine scuttled out of the bedroom. The bedroom door squeaked as she closed it behind her.

Lady Elizabeth waved a hand toward the chesterfield sofa. "Gentlemen do make yourselves comfortable. Ignore my sewing bag; please push it aside."

After proper introductions, we made our way to the sofa and as we sat down, von Stray nonchalantly placed his leather bag next to the dustbin. Convenient to the dustbin stood a small writing desk complete with stationery, pen, ink, and an ink blotter loaded with a fresh blotting sheet. I immediately deduced these items would have no bearing whatsoever in our quest to solve the case.

"I'm delighted, Lady Elizabeth," von Stray began, "to learn you are able to continue sewing. Only now I hope the needle and thread serve as a hobby and not a dangerous venture as it did in former times."

Von Stray was half joke but full earnest regarding Lady Elizabeth's dangerous adventures with her trusty sewing bag. In fact, it wouldn't surprise me if the grayish-green colored sewing bag we now sat next to, saved more lives than the millions of shells fired against opposing trenches. In order to help boost public morale after the War, the government released these following portions of her daring exploits to a citizenship yearning for healthy distraction. Yearning for heroes and heroines. With the aid of a pincushion and flat-head sewing pins, Lady Elizabeth contrived an ingenious method for conveying top-secret information regarding the movements of enemy ships, troops, and aero-plane reconnaissance missions. Risking life and limb, she would slip behind enemy lines, disguise herself as a downcast seamstress and crisscross Germany by train. While traveling she would sew leaving her pincushion in full view for confidants to see. The pins in the pincushion would be arranged in Morse code relaying vital information to her fellow secret agents and ultimately His Majesty.

"I'm afraid I can do little else." Lady Elizabeth held up her right hand, pressed her thumb against her forefinger and waved her hand gracefully as she spoke. "A stitch here a stitch there. An occasional letter or note to a close friend. Dear Catherine is kind enough to post them for me, and keep my desk in order."

Von Stray held up the grayish-green pincushion and jested, "I see your sewing-bag and pincushion are the same color as the German uniform used during the War. Ingenious. I wonder, Lady Elizabeth, could this pincushion be the very one issued to you by the Crown for your war-time service?"

Our gracious host nodded. "Indeed it is, Mr. von Stray. Complete with flat pins for your entertainment."

"I can see that," said my companion, a twinkle sparkled in his left eye. "Ten flat pins organized in a neat pattern as if ready for action."

"You are quite observant, Mr. von Stray. You remind me of Theseus, my American contact during my visits to Germany during the war. I learned through various sources that he had a theatrical background." She paused. A youthful gleam filled her eyes as she lifted the corners of her mouth so slightly the change could be detected by only the keenest of observers. "He used his superior theatrical skills to outfox the enemy on more than one occasion. A master of disguise, you know. Quite the clever man he is…er…was. And quite dashing, too."

Von Stray asked, "Do you know what became of Theseus after the war?"

Lady Elizabeth pulled her quilt closer to her chin. "I'm…not quite sure. When our work was done, we lost contact. The American powers that be felt his real name must remain confidential."

As interested as I was in Lady Elizabeth's espionage adventures and her dashing counterpart Theseus, I couldn't have been more certain that they had no bearing whatsoever on the present matter, so I thought it best to direct my companion back to the purpose of our visit. "Von Stray, perhaps you might like to enquire about the missing pearls?"

"Indeed, Professor. When did you first notice the pearls' disappearance, Lady

Elizabeth?

"Wednesday morning. Catherine cleaned them Tuesday evening and brought

them to me for inspection. Afterward she asked me if I wanted them returned to the safe and I declined, instructing her to place them on top of my writing desk. When I awoke Wednesday morning, they were gone."

"Catherine did as instructed?"

"Most certainly. I saw her place the pearls on the table. They were there when she left."

"Other than yourself, would anyone have access to your bedroom during the night?"

"Massey has a passkey and no one else. He always locks my bedroom door after Catherine delivers my evening glass of warm milk."

"And you are sure he locked the door on the evening in question?"

Lady Elizabeth stifled a yawn. "Yes. Quite sure. He has never failed to do so."

Von Stray rose from the sofa, walked slowly past the writing desk and to the bay windows. "And the windows? I notice they are open now. Who is in charge of ensuring they are shut and locked for the evening?"

"Catherine. I am quite sure she did so."

Von Stray held out his hand in my direction. "Professor, may I borrow your spectacles?"

I find it extremely difficult to hide my consternation when I hear this frequent request coming from my companion. While inspecting minute areas he is in the habit of using my spectacles for a more thorough examination. I stood up and delivered. "Please, von Stray, remember the delicate frames."

He donned the spectacles and then carefully inspected the windows, their frames, and their locking mechanism. Much to my relief he removed my spectacles with care. He then craned his neck out the window as if inspecting the magnolia and surrounding grounds. I was relieved he'd already removed my spectacles and any risk of their untimely plunge to the ground. Returning to the sofa, however, the spectacles slipped out of his normally nimble hands, and tumbled into the waste-bin. He quickly plucked them out and just as rapidly reached into his investigative bag for a linen cloth. After wiping the spectacles clean, he handed them back to me.

Miraculously, they were no worse for wear. "Von Stray! Please be more careful."

"Forgive me, Dilpate," my companion said, folding up the cloth and dropping it back into his bag. He then removed his pipe from his blazer's breast pocket and held it canted as he ventured on with his inquiry. "Lady Elizabeth, apart from the bedroom door and windows, does the room have any other means of entry? Secret passages, for instance?"

"None."

"Could anyone have entered your bedroom without awakening you?"

"I'm a light sleeper and have been after Norman to take care of that infernal door squeak. You heard it did you not, Professor?"

"I most certainly did, Lady Elizabeth. No question it would have awoken you in time to stop the culprit in his tracks."

Von Stray continued. "Lady Elizabeth, you stated that it is your custom to drink warm milk before retiring for the evening. Did you detect any sleeping additive in the milk?"

Lady Elizabeth took a deep breath. "I did not. I can assure you my staff is *above* suspicion. I would have known if my milk had been adulterated."

Von Stray bit down on the stem of his pipe. "How may I ask?"

"My sixth sense! I am familiar with both yours and Professor Dilpate's service in the War, so please don't take offense at my attempt to equate my own small contributions to the fight to your combat experiences. As you know, many credit their survival to a sixth sense. As I traveled throughout Germany, France, Belgium, and even England, there were many instances where I had to rely on my sixth sense. It has never failed me; my existence here today is my proof. My staff and family are beyond reproach. I trust them without exception."

Von Stray nodded. "I understand completely. I wish to raise only one other matter...."

Lady Elizabeth finished his thought. "You are going to ask me about the nexus between the magnolia petals and the missing pearls," she said, while staring at the magnolia tree, speaking in a disconsolate manner. "If that is the case, then Sir Hamilton briefed you fully on the matter as I advised him to. I will not waste anymore time explaining this point. You must speak to my nephew about this case. I know you are aware of his condition, but he can help you. He will be a great asset, von Stray. With just a little push he will lead you to the answer if you allow him. Now, I must take my afternoon nap, but before I do, please open the center drawer of my writing desk. In it you will find a note written by a most desperate individual who left it on the table in place of the pearls. Find the author of the note and you will find the perpetrator."

We accepted these as Lady Elizabeth's final words on the subject and bade her farewell after von Stray retrieved the cryptic note.

In the privacy of our quarters, von Stray and I discussed the case. I didn't bother to hide my concern for our lovely hostess. "I'm afraid our meeting with Lady Elizabeth complicates matters. She gave us nothing more than her sixth sense and instructions to take her nephew into our confidence. Smethwick is right, the poor lad is suffering from shell-shock and I fear there's nothing we can do for him."

Von Stray ignited a long-needed pipe and said between bursts of smoke, "Come now, Professor let's not give up on the lad. As far as her sixth-sense theory goes, you logged enough hours in the War to give it some credence. In fact many, myself included, credit it as fact—not theory."

"I'm with you, von Stray, but to a point. Her loyalty to staff is commendable, yet it's as plain as a pikestaff that a staff member adulterated her milk with a sedative, slipped into her bedroom, and stole the pearls. In order to solve this case, we must apply sound logical analysis."

Von Stray held up the mysterious note found on Lady Elizabeth's writing desk. "I'm glad we are in logical agreement, Dilpate, for I can assure you that the individual who arranged the pearls' disappearance is operating on a superior level we have never before encountered."

As my dear friend uttered these words, I gazed out a bedroom window at the remarkable view of high cliffs leading to and surrounding the lighthouse. A sense of foreboding washed over me. I feared this beacon of hope and the narrow stretch of land—we would soon come to know as the 'Devil's Plank'—connecting Gurnet Village and the lighthouse, would ultimately lure us into a sea of perpetual darkness.

VII: Mysterious Impressions

As von Stray and I began to examine the anonymous note left on Lady Elizabeth's desk, we heard the rumble of Sir Ambrose's automobile sweeping up from the forecourt. We looked out a window from our quarters and saw him leap out of the contraption and dash toward the front door.

Von Stray put a hand on my shoulder. "Let's see if we can elicit Sir Ambrose's assistance in analyzing this mysterious missive the culprit exchanged for the pearls."

I remained doubtful. "Von Stray, as much as I detest this Smethwick bloke, I'm afraid he's correct. The boy needs more than a little push. He has suffered an irreversible shell-shock from the War."

My companion was insistent. "Then perhaps a big push is in order. Lady Elizabeth has given us our marching orders. We owe her our allegiance."

I conceded without hesitation. "Indeed, von Stray. My apologies. Our duty is to Lady Elizabeth, but I insist we give her no false hope."

My companion nodded. "I couldn't agree more, Dilpate."

When we arrived on the ground floor and were greeted by Sir Ambrose, I was flabbergasted. I couldn't believe this was the same young man we had met earlier. When he had leaped out of the motorcar, he had scampered for the front door in such a hurry I hadn't noticed his change of attire. He now looked every bit the working fisherman from head to foot. A tattered wool sweater, battered trousers, and scuffed rubber Wellies stretching up to his knees. I regret to say the odor of the day's catch completed his attire.

He acknowledged us with a wide smile and firm handshake. "Gentlemen.

Thank you for waiting. Sorry for the delay. Had to help the crew bundle-up a haul of whiting for market. Let's get on with our investigation, shall we? As you know, every moment we delay petals slip from the tree and so trickles the fate of Suckling."

I should have been astounded but wasn't. Smethwick and I were right all along. All this young man needed was a hard day's work on the docks and he snapped out of his shell-shock.

If von Stray was as astonished, he didn't reveal so. "Your assistance, Sir Ambrose is much appreciated and needed. Is there a quiet place where we can pool our collective knowledge about the case?"

"Off to my study, men. Double-time. We can sport the oak and maintain complete secrecy. Henceforth, no more of this 'Sir' nonsense. Plain old 'Ambrose' will do."

Inside Ambrose's gilt-and-tasseled study he gave us a brief tour. Each wall was strewn with reminders of past sporting victories—hunting horns, prized niblicks, cricket bats, foils, and equestrian trophies. The few trophy plates I read were dated pre-War. Prior to the War he had undoubtedly been an exceptional sportsman—his bright future as Lord of the Manor all but assured.

After the tour he and von Stray lit pipes. My learned friend then produced the mysterious note left on Lady Elizabeth's writing desk. I shuddered as I read its ghoulish contents.

Say farewell, manor lass
To all you know
Each sun does pass
Closer reaps what you sow
Kindred spirits no more
No eyes folklore
All past is due
Death in the air
Everyone gone ado
Ladyship do despair

The note was written in black ink in a most distinctive script. We held the document up to the light and although the paper appeared to be of a heavy weight, no manufacturer's paper bond appeared.

Von Stray said to Ambrose, "Do you recognize the handwriting?"

Ambrose studied the document quite closely. After much intense concentration he shook his head. "I do not." He snapped his fingers. "By thunder I've got it! The culprit disguised his writing."

"Excellent point," von Stray said, crediting Ambrose. "What about the paper? Do you know of anyone who might use this type?"

Ambrose studied the paper closely, but again was unable to name a source. He paced the room and then snapped his fingers. "Gentlemen, perhaps we will find clues in the words themselves."

"Most ingenious," said von Stray. It did not take me long to realize von Stray was giving Ambrose the opportunity to take lead on the case. Von Stray picked up the letter and studied it carefully before handing it to me. He asked, "How is your German, Professor?"

"German? A bit rusty I'm afraid."

He handed the note to Ambrose. "And your German?"

Ambrose shook his head. "Find me some Morse code and I'm your man. As far as German goes, I'm afraid the word 'halt' is about the extent of my vocabulary. Other than a few words one would be reluctant to introduce at one of auntie's social gatherings."

"I see," said von Stray, smiling as he snatched up his leather bag. "I must leave you gentlemen for the time being as I perform a small task. I'm convinced that Ambrose's theory about the poem being a cipher is correct. When properly decoded I believe it will provide the key to solving this puzzling matter. In my absence,

perhaps you men will work together to unravel its meaning."

"We will do so," said Ambrose with great excitement. "You can count on us."

I sensed von Stray was withholding from me a vital piece of information in the case. Further, I knew without a doubt that all this nonsense about knowing German was simply a pretext to keep us busy while he went off alone to carry out his mysterious task. Nevertheless, for Lady Elizabeth's sake, I reluctantly agreed with my companion's scheme. "Yes…of course, von Stray, but perhaps—"

"Thank you, Professor. I know everything is in good hands." With that, von Stray dashed out of the study leather bag in hand.

For the next half hour or so Ambrose and I put our shoulders to the helm but remained adrift. I blamed von Stray for putting the notion foremost in our thoughts that somehow the German language was the key to decoding the puzzle.

With our wits now at the end of their rope, Ambrose came up with a sensible suggestion. "Did it occur to you, Professor that the author of the note intended it as a dodge?"

I raised my spectacles. "What do you mean?"

"While we're here shilly-shallying trying to close the stable door, the horses have already been stolen."

"I see. Quite ingenious. There's *nothing* to decode. The note's a red herring intended to distract us from following the threads which lead to legitimate clues."

Ambrose gripped my arm in friendship. "Precisely."

"I'm shocked von Stray did not think of this," I murmured.

"That's because he doesn't know of the clues I discovered before your arrival."

In less time than it takes to tell, we were under the great magnolia tree and inspecting its immediate grounds. I have to say it was at this time I couldn't have been more proud of Ambrose. I never doubted that like his great-great grandfather Sir Moreleans, he would overcome his troubles and live a vigorous and productive life. His analysis of the case was as impressive as anything von Stray could deduce.

"Look up," said Ambrose, pointing to Lady Elizabeth's open bay windows. "Directly above is auntie's bedroom. Now look here." He pointed to a soft bed of soil along the foundation under her window. "Watch your footing, Professor. We don't want the area disturbed. Note these two square impressions," he said, removing a small notebook to consult. "They measure sixteen inches apart. The impressions themselves measure two inches by four inches. Each impression measures to a depth of approximately three inches."

The impressions were plain as a pikestaff, and I couldn't imagine how von Stray had missed them when he looked out of Lady Elizabeth's windows. Her bedroom was approximately twenty-five feet from the ground and the impressions could easily have been spotted from that elevation. It's possible the foundation ivy obstructed his view, although I can't see how since the impressions were easily two feet off of the foundation and thus, extending far beyond the drip line of the ivy.

Ambrose snapped his notebook shut and smiled. "Now, Professor. Can you think of any object that might make such impressions?"

I thought for a moment. "It's inescapable—a ladder!"

"Right-ho! Moreover, based on the depths of the impressions—I won't bore you with my mathematical conclusions—the prowler using our mysterious vanishing ladder weighs approximately 14 stone."

"Well played! You're on track to solving this bewildering puzzle before von Stray."

He held up his index finger. "On track is right, Professor." Ambrose crouched down and carefully swept away a few ivy leaves that had undoubtedly fallen to the ground as a result of some playful house sparrows. "Look at the deep footprints around the ladder impressions."

"Brilliant discovery, Ambrose. Now all we have to do is find the owner of the shoes and we will have found the culprit."

"I already have. Size eleven brogues and they fit into these shoeprints as they say: 'like a glove.'"

"Smethwick!"

I must have shouted his name because no sooner had I done so than Smethwick appeared from the forecourt. "Quiet. This isn't one of your jollifications, Ambrose. Her Ladyship is napping. Why are you two pottering about under her window anyway?"

Ambrose raised his chin. "We might ask you the same question...cousin."

Smethwick leaned into him. "Oh you might—might you!"

Ambrose took a step back and swallowed a couple of times.

Smethwick took full advantage of the retreat. "Take off that filthy garb and get properly dressed for tea. You look like a haberdasher's nightmare. This isn't a ploughman's luncheon."

While Ambrose readied for tea I provided von Stray with a full report of our investigative findings. For my money the irrefutable evidence was all in. The only thing left to do was to confront Smethwick and give him a bit of the old sabre-rattling until he revealed where he'd hidden the pearls.

"Excellent work, Dilpate. I suspected something of this nature. I haven't quite figured out how Smethwick fits into this baffling case, nevertheless, perhaps a few artful questions during tea will bring us closer to the answer."

I was aghast. "While you were off with your mysterious task, Ambrose and I solved the case. We need only confront Smethwick with the evidence. He climbed up the ladder, gained entry through Her Ladyship's window, and stole the pearls."

"Perhaps you are correct, Dilpate. Many men have gone to the gallows on less evidence. Just what role Smethwick may have played in their disappearance I cannot say with complete certainty at this time. I must advise you, however, that my examination of the window locks and sash revealed no signs of tampering. I know only that our quest for more clues must continue before I make my final conclusions."

Although I was quite certain the evidence Ambrose and I uncovered against Smethwick was conclusive, I knew better than to challenge the great detective's unique analytic methods of crime detection. Accordingly, I spent the remaining time before tea putting order to my moustache, which was in desperate need of grooming.

VIII: Time is of the Essence

Catherine held tea outside on the large bluestone patio located in the back of the manor where we had a clear view of the distant lighthouse. Lady Elizabeth was unable to join us; however, despite a few dark clouds drifting up from the southeast, the afternoon sun warmed and brightened our spirits in her absence. Catherine put on an exquisite serving of delicious smoked salmon sandwiches, cucumber sandwiches, and a most delightful homemade German bee sting cake. Ambrose looked every bit the young gentlemen; unfortunately, his high sprits during our investigation had suddenly waned. Despite the friendly overtures from von Stray and I—and especially from young Catherine—he barely communicated during tea.

Adding further to my concerns regarding the direction in which von Stray was taking the investigation was his random questioning of Smethwick. As far as I could see, his interrogatories had nothing to do with the case.

Von Stray placed his teacup gently onto its saucer and said, "I trust you had a robust walk this afternoon, Mr. Smethwick?"

"I did indeed. Peaceful stroll along the beach to the lighthouse and returned by that narrow neck of land these simple villagers call the Devil's Plank. Something about evil spirits popping up at night and yanking unsuspecting strollers over the cliff and into the sea. Utter foolishness. Isn't that right, Ambrose or are you a subscriber of this childish superstition?"

Ambrose gazed at his tea while answering. "I've climbed all the cliffs I'll ever climb."

Smethwick looked as if he were about to chop Ambrose off at the knees when von Stray came to the rescue. "Superstitions or not, you are to be commended, Mr. Smethwick for successfully negotiating the Plank, I'm sure. I was sorry to learn of your War injury. Where did you serve? Perhaps we shared lodgings in close proximity."

Smethwick bit into a smoked salmon sandwich prior to answering. "Er... well...the usual places...France...Belgium. All over you know. Ghastly conditions, you know...er...mud and blood and all that. Not worth revisiting."

"I see. So you were really in the thick of it indeed."

Smethwick scooped up a cucumber sandwich this time. "Ahh...thick indeed. Quite thick. It was so long ago and as I said, I don't wish to discuss it, von Stray. You understand. More tea?"

Before von Stray could respond Ambrose pushed himself away from the table and started taking measured steps toward the old stable. It was partially obstructed by a thick hedgerow. He then began to sprint directly for the hedgerow and in a most amazing leap hurtled over the three-foot wall of shrubbery. Moments later we heard the rumble of his slick motor-car and just as swiftly we watched it race away from the manor.

Smethwick shook his fist. "And that, gentlemen, is the result of to the manor born!" He grabbed his walking stick and with great effort stood up from his chair. He turned his upper body toward the ocean and while shaking his right fist at it thundered, "The drums of war have reached a fever pitch." His short soliloquy completed, he faced the table and before making his departure, said glibly, "I will see you at dinner, gentlemen. I wish you good hunting with your hopeless endeavor."

"I think we are quite finished with tea, Dilpate," said von Stray, as he watched Smethwick disappear into the house.

"But I haven't finished my bee sting cake," I protested. "I haven't tasted one this authentic since before the War."

"I'm afraid you'll have to sacrifice your last bite. We must continue our investigation."

"Where?"

"To the garden-house. I believe the head gardener Theodore may be able to provide us with a great deal of information in helping us solve this increasingly strange case."

"What could he possibly know of the pearls' disappearance?" I said, stalling in order to gobble my last bite of bee sting.

Von Stray was on his feet and in a few swift moves had his pipe fully charged and his leather investigative bag in hand. "The answer to your question will largely depend upon how much information he can tell us about your mysterious ladder and purported prowler!"

We found Theodore in the greenhouse potting some geraniums. He was an elderly gentleman of a slight compact build—much like my own—with a jaunty note about him. When he saw us coming, he turned to face us. I was shocked to see he was missing his left arm at the elbow. In spite of it not even the fussiest critic—with the exception of the overgrown magnolia—could find anything derivative about his care for the estate's grounds. His dedication to duty under such conditions immediately credited him as a proud man who found joy and meaning in his day-to-day duties. Even his impressive military-looking grey moustache boasted tidy order.

He opened our discussion without introduction as if his knowledge of the ladder was scripted. "Good afternoon, gents," he said, before removing his floppy beret sporting a Sevenoaks Regiment cap badge dating back to the Second Afghan War. "Von Stray and Professor Dilpate is it? Theodore Connolly 'ead gardener Suckling. Been expectin' you, blokes…er…gents 'ere about the ladder, what? 'Bout time. Come on over 'ere. Let's get on with it. These poor geraniums are anxious to get into their new 'ome."

He led us into the garden-house. "Now, gents 'ere's the ladder that peaked Sir Ambrose's interest. A wooden jobber as you can see, and it's the one I always use to trim down the ivy. Awful nuisance the ivy. Mind of its own. If you don't beat it back, it'll climb up and swallow up the 'ole 'ouse. Now, you don't 'ave to be a detective—no offense, men—to see these butt ends 'ere on the ladder are the ones that punched those awful dirty 'oles in my garden beds under 'er Ladyship's bedroom windows. Soil on the ladder's dry now, but still a little caked up on the butt ends in question. See? Okay then. Now, you gents know me well and if you think I would return a ladder to my garden-'ouse in this filthy condition…well…then my guess is that you don't know me as you claims. Why just look at them two Rudge-Whitworth push-bicycle specimens against the wall. Sparkle like the first day they was new."

Von Stray and I exchanged glances. It didn't escape our notice that our strange, black-bearded friend from the passenger train rode off from the Ramsgate station with the same brand of push-bicycle.

"When Sir Ambrose and his lady friend take them out for a spree," Theodore continued, "the contraptions comes back looking like they been dragged through a quagmire. Not going to dirty up my garden 'ouse with those filthy contraptions I tell 'em. They 'ad better be spotless and then some."

Theodore paused for a moment and leaned into me in a confidential manner. "Got to keep after the young ones what slack on the old ways eh, Professor. And further, I might add on top of the aforementioned—with no less importance 'erewith—if you think I would leave 'er Ladyship's garden beds looking like a pack of foxhounds got a 'old of old Mr. Fox there, then I repeat myself that you, blokes…er…gents don't know me from Adam as you claims."

Von Stray took advantage of our jaunty friend's pause. "I take it then, Theodore that someone removed the ladder from the garden-house and used it without your permission?"

Theodore placed his beret over his heart. "On me 'onor, Mr. von Stray. On me 'onor…I would never do nuthin' against 'er Ladyship's wishes."

"I believe you, sir," said von Stray. "I won't impose on your time any further except if we may, to take a few measurements of the ladder."

Theodore nodded. "By all means, sir if you think it will 'elp 'er Ladyship."

Von Stray reached into his leather bag and removed his folding rule. He unfolded a few of its pivoting hinges, and measured the width of the ladder. "Sixteen inches wide, Dilpate. This confirms Ambrose's measurement. Now for the length of the ladder."

Von Stray unfolded the rest of the rule's pivoting hinges and together we measured the length of the ladder. "Fifteen feet on my end," I told my companion. Anticipating his next measure, I volunteered the measurement of the portion of ladder extending beyond the top rung. "And one foot from the top rung to ladder's end." The measurements of the ladder shot through me like a lightening bolt. Not only did they shatter my Smethwick theory but created a more plausible suspect—Ambrose.

Von Stray quickly folded up the ruler and returned it to his bag. "As I suspected, Dilpate. The ladder extends to about the same height of the house ivy." Von Stray turned to Theodore. "Thank you, Theodore you have been most helpful indeed. I will be sure to inform Her Ladyship of your assistance and devotion to duty."

Theodore refitted his beret and raised his chin. "Most kind of you, Mr. von Stray. Will there be anything further?"

"I think not. We have imposed on your beautiful geraniums long enough!"

After meeting with Theodore, we posted up at the magnolia tree. By this time, dark clouds cluttered the sky and increasing winds striped more and more flower petals off the tree. I warned my friend. "Von Stray, the wind is plucking the flowers off the tree!"

"I can see that, Professor. All the more reason to examine the evidence now before Mother Nature washes it away."

"Yes," I said, looking up at the sky, "I think we can expect torrential rains."

Using his folding rule and my spectacles he had once again managed to wrestle from me, von Stray inspected the ladder and footprint impressions. "I complement you and Ambrose on your thoroughness, Dilpate," he said, returning my spectacles and then dropping the folding rule into his bag.

"I'm baffled, von Stray," I said, pulling my hat on tighter against the intensifying winds. "At fifteen feet the ladder falls significantly short of Lady Elizabeth's windows. They must be twenty-five feet above ground. Even if Smethwick managed to stand on the top rung of the ladder—a foot lower than the ladder itself—at his own height of approximately six feet he'd still be about five feet short of the window ledge. Considering his damaged leg, he couldn't possibly make the scramble into Her Ladyship's bedroom."

"I agree, Dilpate. I'm afraid it becomes significantly less probable when we consider the ladder's maximum reach becomes lower still when propped diagonally against the house."

"Yes, that would shave off a couple of feet."

"Exactly, Dilpate. The height of the ladder essentially dictates the height at which Theodore periodically trims down the ivy as it creeps up the side of the house. Let's suppose for a moment our prowler props the ladder against the house. The butt ends of the top of the ladder would lean against the ivy. The pressure of the ladder combined with the weight of the climber would undoubtedly disturb the ivy and explain the fallen ivy leaves Ambrose swept away from the fresh footprints."

"But surely," said I, taking his supposition in a more logical direction, "even in the dark the culprit would know the ladder fell far too short. Why bother climbing the ladder at that point? The only possible explanation is that Ambrose, with his superior athletic skills was somehow able to scale the remaining portion of foundation wall, reach the window ledge, and ultimately gain entry through the bay windows."

My companion rubbed the back of his neck. "Possibly, Dilpate. How then would you explain Ambrose's conclusion that these are Smethwick's footprints at the base of the ladder?"

I thought for a moment. "Come to think of it there is only Ambrose's word these are Smethwick's footprints. I've got it! When Smethwick leaves his shoes outside his bedroom door this evening for polishing, we'll borrow them and conduct our own independent inquiry."

"There's no guarantee he will do so, Dilpate, yet I agree with you that we must independently corroborate Ambrose's alleged findings. I believe there may be a more efficient way to see whether in fact these mysterious footprints bring us a step closer to solving this intriguing case."

"How?"

He quickly scooped his bag without bothering to fasten it shut. "Later, Dilpate," he said, pointing left to a bridleway. "This path leads toward the beach. We haven't a moment to spare! Time and tide wait for no man," he shouted as he sprang toward the path.

IX: A Quarter Moon Afoot

I clung to my companion's heels as he set a furious pace down the path toward the cliff overlooking the beach. At the cliff's edge, we double-stepped it down a steep winding set of stairs leading to the beach. Having served in the Royal Navy, von Stray didn't have to remind me about rising tides. High tide was on the march and the Straight of Dover was making quick work of consuming the remaining patch of beach. I could see by the saltwater stains and seaweed clinging to the foot of the high rocky cliff that the ocean was in the habit of swallowing the beach whole at high tide.

I shouted over the intensifying winds. "Careful, von Stray! Don't wander too far from the stairs. The tide is quickly rising and if we venture too far there's no turning back unless you're prepared to swim to France or scale the cliff—it must be a hundred feet high or more."

"Only people who live indoors think in terms of bad weather, Dilpate! We must follow the clues wherever they lead us." The great detective looked to his right in the direction of the lighthouse, which stood on its high bluff at least a mile away. He removed his field glasses from his bag, and focused them toward the bluff. "It looks as if there's higher ground at the foot of the lighthouse. If we hurry we can make it there before the tide envelopes the beach."

He shoved the field glasses back into his bag and went off like a shot toward our new objective. As he ran he kept looking down at the beach's surface never explaining to me what he expected to find. The crashing waves seemed to be gunning for us with every stride. By the time we safely reached the high ground area of beach below the lighthouse, our path had been reduced to a foot of running space between wave and cliff. I was also quite mindful of the increasing gale-force winds and, as a result, the increasing size of the surging waves.

After I caught my breath I said to von Stray, "Thank heavens we made it, but I fear we'll be trapped here until the tide recedes."

"Indeed, Dilpate. Just in time too. I was afraid the turbulent sea would wash away the evidence."

"Wash away us more likely. Those breakers would have pounded us into the rocky cliff at ramming speed and smashed us into smithereens before dragging our sodden remains out to sea." I looked behind me as foamy waves now exploded against the cliff. "What evidence?"

"Fresh shoeprints, Professor. You will recall how during tea Smethwick said his walk took him to the lighthouse this afternoon. If true, I surmised he might have left shoeprint impressions in the wet sand. See here, old man," said von Stray, pointing to the sand. "A dozen footprints have thus far been spared by the tide. We must complete our examination before the tide covers this remaining portion of high ground and washes away our clues."

I looked down and saw a set of footprints leading up as far as a large hunk of flat granite. The granite fed into a flight of stone stairs leading up to the lighthouse. Clumps of ragged seaweed clung to its base. The great detective was right; the tide would soon reach the granite slab.

"Quickly, Dilpate, your spectacles before the tide laps the shoeprints into oblivion."

While removing my spectacles I was compelled to protest. "When will you get a magnifying glass, von Stray?"

He took the spectacles and crouched down to examine a right shoeprint. He was careful not to disturb the surrounding sand. "Why look under one magnifying glass when I can use both eyes belonging to my able colleague? Why just think of how many rare beetles you have carefully inspected and classified through these remarkable lenses!" Completing his examination, he stood up and returned my spectacles. "As usual, my dear friend you and your specs have not let me down."

"What is it, von Stray?"

"As I suspected the right heel has a distinct gash shaped like a quarter moon. When I examined the shoeprints left conveniently under Her Ladyship's window, I observed the same distinctive gash. It was there the whole time for the trained eye to see."

"By Jehoshaphat, von Stray! If these shoeprints are indeed Smethwick's, then we can undoubtedly place him at the ladder. If Inspector Renyalds of Scotland Yard were here, he'd certainly say this settles the hash."

"Yes, but how often has the good inspector been mislead by his propensity to rush to judgment? As I have warned many times, Professor: 'Cases relying solely on circumstantial evidence have a tendency to invite false inferences.' The matching shoeprints do demonstrate clear and convincing evidence placing Smethwick within the proximity of the missing pearls, yet even if true, I'm afraid we've exchanged one knotty problem for another."

"What do you mean?"

"Look at the shoeprints closely."

I did so and observed nothing in addition to what von Stray had already deduced from them.

"If you recall," he explained, "when Smethwick departed for his walk this afternoon, he held his walking stick in his left hand. He even tapped his left shoe with the tip of his walking stick claiming the foot had been injured in the War. Again, at tea he held the stick on his left side. Look again, Dilpate." I did so. "Note the conspicuous series of puncture holes in the sand. Three remain leading up to the granite slab where the shoeprints end."

"Von Stray, the holes are on the right side of the shoeprints!"

"Precisely, Dilpate. Equally noteworthy is the absence of such puncture holes on the left side!"

X: The Pea Fogger

"Great Scott!" I exclaimed, clamping down my cap against a sudden gust. "Smethwick is an imposter."

"I suspected so when during tea he provided evasive responses regarding his alleged military service."

I looked at the incoming tide and its ferocious breakers. Soon they would be further augmented by swirling and increasing gale-force winds. The relentless surf clawed at our heels as if determined to pull us into the grip of its powerful undertow. "We must hurry up the bluff to the lighthouse, von Stray."

We leapt onto the granite block and watched as a crashing wave erased Smethwick's remaining footprints.

"Say goodbye to our evanescent evidence, Dilpate."

"Yes," I lamented. "Unfortunately, the heavy rains will wash away his footprints under the windows as well."

My dear friend held up his leather bag and tapped its side. "Undoubtedly, Dilpate. Fortunately, I carry with me another bit of evidence I intend to share with you at the appropriate time. Meanwhile, let's hurry up to the lighthouse and take shelter before the inevitable tempest."

No sooner had my friend spoke these words when a thunderous crash caught our attention. We looked up to the rim of the cliff and a huge wedge of earth carrying a mature oak tree yielded to the sudden torrential rains, slid from the edge of the cliff, and tumbled into the boiling surf. The remaining trees lining the rim of the cliff clung on for dear life to mere scrubby tufts of earth while portions of their root systems, exposed by erosion, hung downward like vines toward the sea.

Von Stray said, "With rain and tide working in tandem, the day will soon come when Mother Nature breaches the Devil's Plank, and converts the area into an island. Hurry, Dilpate, to the lighthouse!"

With redoubled urgency we climbed 147 steps up to the lighthouse located approximately 100 feet above the ocean. By the time we arrived at the top, torrential rains were slanting down on the tiny bluff of fastidiously maintained lighthouse grounds. We ran toward the beacon at breakneck speed and as soon as we reached the entrance door it swung open. A salty-looking gentleman sporting grey side-whiskers, and a bulky wool turtleneck sweater came into our line of vision. Our rescuer dragged us inside and out of harm's way. After shaking off the rain we introduced ourselves to our new friend, Austin Quinby, lighthouse keeper.

He pointed the mashed stem of his yellow-stained meerschaum pipe at the corner of his right eye. "I keep a keen eye, gents. Saw you sloggin' up the stairs. Well, I'm afraid it's eat mutton, and say nuttin' for you two. You'll 'ave to ride out the storm 'ere. Fog's thick as pea soup. Means you 'ave more steps a'ead of you. I 'ave to get back to my post up top and if you want a spot of tea and mutton stew, I suggest you follow, but quick."

I would have followed the old shellback another 1,000 steps for a cup of tea and bowl of mutton stew. With each winding step we took toward the top of the tower, the delicious aroma of stew grew stronger. I privately thanked my Indian club exercises for keeping me in tip-top condition to help make the climb.

In Quinby's quarters directly below the lighthouse's beacon he survived on the simplest of amenities and yet the man seemed to want for nothing. The cramped, but homey accommodations suggested our new friend lived with more contentment than the occupants of a dozen castles. I had met many great men like him during my service in the Royal Navy and felt instant comradeship.

Quinby stirred a small crock of stew further exciting its yummy aroma. "Ahh, she's ready, gents. You timed your escape from this pestering squall perfect."

Von Stray said, "You couldn't have expected us, Quinby. Please enjoy your small portion of stew without us intruding."

It took all my willpower to side with von Stray. "Yes, I insisted. Biscuits and tea is all we require."

"Nonsense, gents. Crock is full to the brim she is. I was 'oping my new acquaintance would return for another visit, but 'e must be caught up battening down the 'atches."

Quinby kept a steady eye on the ocean while we consumed a bowl of his mouthwatering stew flanked with a few rations of hardtack.

"Aye, lads," Quinby lamented, after he'd slurped a generous portion of stew, "'eavy fog's rollin' in but quick."

Von Stray balanced a hunk of mutton onto his spoon. "I wonder, Quinby if we share the same acquaintance—a Mr. Edward Smethwick?"

Quinby blew on a spoonful of hot broth and shook his head. "Didn't give a surname. Gave a name of Julius. I don't ask a man too many questions. Interesting bloke. Said the view up 'ere inspired the tempest in 'im. Then 'e looked out this 'ere window and said as if the ocean was 'is theater and the waves 'is spectators, 'I shall no more to sea, to sea.'"

Von Stray continued to press our new friend. "What did this gentlemen look like?"

"Big strikin' bloke sportin' a thick black beard. Can't give you more than that," Quinby said, jerking his head in the direction of the sea. "'Ave to keep a keen eye on my duties."

I was thunder-struck. "Von Stray! He's described that strange man from the train perfectly. What would he be doing in Smethwick's shoes? Unless of course they both happen to have the same gash on their right heel."

The great detective was impressed with my inescapable logical conclusion. "We have a little more work to do on our hypothesis, Dilpate before we connect Quinby's guest to the shoeprints found on the beach. Tell me, Quinby, did your friend carry a walking stick?"

Quinby pulled thoughtfully on his pipe. "Yes and no. Must of left it outside when 'e arrived. When 'e departed I glanced down at 'im from up 'ere in my perch. 'E was twirling a stick as 'e strolled down the path back to the village.

A dapper fellow 'e was."

Von Stray sprang to his feet, reached both hands into his bag, and without removing them, wrapped a handy oilskin around a mysterious object. "Dilpate we must investigate this peculiar bit of news at once."

Quinby bit hard into the stem of his pipe and spoke through his teeth. "'Old on, gents. Can't cut and run 'til this storm passes. Only got two points of travel out of 'ere. Can't go by the beach until low tide and in these surges the water's right up against the cliff even after tide change. With nighttime on the drop and in this pea fogger on the brood, if you try to negotiate the thin plank of land connecting this 'ere lighthouse to the village, you'll be overboard and into Davy Jones' locker quicker than a tub of six-day-old chum. They don't call that evil pathway the 'Devil's Plank' for nothin'. A most 'orrible trap for the unwary she is." He paused for a moment and looked out a window in the direction of the Plank. A thick fog framed the window obliterating virtually all visibility. Finally, he removed his pipe and, using its stem, tapped the window. "More than one good man 'as disappeared over them cliffs in a pea fogger."

XI: The Devil's Plank

I swallowed and then looked at von Stray. We didn't have to say a word to know what each other was thinking. Only a fool would ignore the old shellback's warning, nonetheless duty called.

I repeated the words von Stray had said to me a short time ago. "What was it you said earlier, von Stray, 'Only people who live indoors think in terms of bad weather'?"

"We haven't a moment to lose, Dilpate. We must make for Suckling post haste!"

Quinby shook his head. "You'll be killed, gentlemen."

My companion placed a hand on our host's shoulder. "We thank you for your hospitality and concern, Quinby, but we must try. With a little faith, luck, and caution we'll steer a true course."

"You'll need more than them things, my friend." Quinby pivoted, opened a small wooden chest, and pulled out a length of ancient hemp rope about eight feet long. "Each take an end of this rope and 'old it on your journey. Otherwise, you'll separate in the fog. 'Ere, I'll tie a knot on each end so it won't slip from your 'and."

After an exchange of compliments with Quinby, we began our treacherous mile-long walk along the Devil's Plank. Von Stray keeps an electric torch in his investigative bag, but its light beam proved useless against the thick curtain of fog, so back into his bag it went. He then fastened the bag shut. It wasn't long before I regretted not taking the old shellback's advice. Fog and night immediately consumed us, and I couldn't see a hand in front of me, but there was no turning back.

Per our arrangement von Stray led the way. I privately thanked Quinby for his rope idea to link us together. We moved at a sluggish crawl through the muck and after about an hour I venture to guess we'd trudged no more than a quarter-mile. Here I felt the rope slack suddenly. Von Stray had stopped in his tracks.

"Hold fast, Dilpate," my friend commanded.

"What's the matter?"

"Listen."

I listened for a moment. "All I hear is howling winds and rain." Von Stray didn't respond. I tugged the rope. "Von Stray…?" No response. A second later I heard a thundering crash about a stone's throw away.

My friend broke his silence. "Recognize that sound, Dilpate? I venture to guess more earth is toppling into the sea. I fear the Devil's Plank is becoming narrower with each raindrop. We must take every precaution."

I tightened my grip around the rope as we bucked forward and, after a few yards, with thunder-clap surprise, I heard a loud sloshing sound, and the rope instantly tightened. Maintaining my firm grip, the rope yanked me forward as if I'd unexpectedly hooked Jonah's whale, and I fell prostrate to the ground. The earth had suddenly given under von Stray's feet like a trapdoor and he dropped over the cliff. Fortunately, we had both held onto our respective ends of the rope, but his weight dragged me over the slippery mud like a sled down a steep icy slope. I would have flown over the cliff with him but for a convenient small tree I was able to hook my free arm around. The young tree was anchored in by its root system, yet it was quickly losing its own fight against gravity.

"Von Stray," I shouted, "hold on, old man. I'll pull while you climb up the rope hand-over-hand. I'm holding onto a tree. If you can reach its root system, grab hold, and I'll pull you over the rim of the cliff."

"Hold fast, Dilpate. Watch your head, old man."

A second later I could feel a heavy object hurtle past my head. "What in blazes was that?"

"My investigative bag. Rather nice brandy in there."

"For Heaven's sake will you forget your bag and climb!"

No sooner had I given my command when another object fluttered over my head. "Now what the Devil was that?"

"My hat."

"For the love of Saint Peter are you quite through shucking your garments or shall I hum a few burlesque tunes?"

"Quite through, old man. Shall we…?"

As I pulled and von Stray climbed, the tree's root system unexpectedly shifted, and a bushel of mud spilled over the cliff. Even as I slid closer to the rim, I adjusted my weight as best I could and continued to pull the rope. "Keep trying, von Stray."

"It's no use, Dilpate. I'm afraid it's the devil take hindmost. Save yourself. If I keep bobbing my weight as I pull, I fear the tree will uproot and we'll both fall to our doom."

"Never, von Stray. Keep climbing! You must try."

"Dilpate…?"

"What is it now, von Stray—shall I expect a busted suspender to come my way? Climb, old man!"

"Fair harbors, Professor, never has a man had a more faithful companion."

And with these final words from my dear friend the rope slackened completely.

XII: The Cliff Hanger

"Von Stray! Von Stray!" to no avail I yelled to him. Without regard for my own safety I scrambled around for von Stray's bag and when I found it, I quickly removed his electric torch and cast its beam over the rim's edge; it proved useless. The beam only highlighted the fog and further blinded my vision. Nevertheless, I refused to abandon my friend and continued to search and shout his name for what must have been hours. At some point, I would have no way of knowing when, I passed out from utter exhaustion.

I awoke early the next morning stupefied. For a moment I held an unfocused hypnotic gaze at the golden spangles of sunshine shimmering on the ocean while listening to the haunting, wailing shrieks of seagulls. When I reached for my handkerchief in order to wipe the mud splatter and moisture off my spectacle's lenses, I felt something clutched in my hand. I looked down and saw not only was I an untidy, muddy heap, but that I still held Quinby's length of rope. A sudden shock bolted through me before gathering my senses and remembering von Stray. On all fours I scrambled over to the cliff's edge and craned my neck over its rim. His remains were nowhere to be found. My friend and colleague—the great, celebrated detective Henry von Stray—had been claimed by the sea with no more concern than a hunk of driftwood never to return.

I stood up, looked out over the cliff, and shouted to the sea, "Farewell, von Stray. I shall solve this case no matter what the cost."

"Good morning, Professor," said another voice—von Stray's! "And what a beautiful morning it is indeed."

"Von Stray!" I exclaimed, darting away from the cliff's edge and nearly slipping over for my efforts. I ran to him and gripped both his shoulders. "You're alive…you're…not *dead.* But…I felt you let go of the rope? Have I gone balmy or are you really alive!"

"My sincerest apologies, Dilpate," he replied, dabbing his forehead with a blood-soaked handkerchief. "Before letting go of the rope my sixth sense told me to feel for a web of root systems with my right foot and good fortune was with me. I threaded my foot through a crossing of roots and taking the only chance we had, I let go of the rope and fell backward. Much to my relief the roots held onto my foot, but as I struck the cliff, my head spun and hit a protruding rock. I was knocked unconscious. When I finally awoke, I pulled myself up and climbed up the roots using them like the ratlines of an old sailing vessel. Lord Nelson would have been proud."

I wiped my spectacle lenses as best I could with my own sodden handkerchief and demanded, "By Jove! Why didn't you tell me your plan?"

"There was no time to argue. I knew you wouldn't let go of the rope and we would've both been lost."

"Nonsense," I cried, now coiling up the rope and placing it into von Stray's investigative bag. I sometimes preserve these important historical artifacts from our adventures and display them in our lodgings' sitting room. "I've the grip of a blacksmith and I had a solid purchase on my fine little oak tree."

He pressed the handkerchief down on his forehead. "It wouldn't be the first time an oak tree saved an Englishman, but I'm afraid in this case your fledgling oak was nearly done for and had a strong enough hold to save one soul from a rocky grave but not two."

I wanted to debate the point further, but a more pressing matter concerned me. "Let me have a look at that head of yours." Von Stray lifted the handkerchief off his forehead, and I inspected his wound. "It's stopped bleeding. Nasty bump indeed, but I've received worse from an off balance left sweep I once performed during one of my Indian club exercise regimens. You'll live."

"Thank you, Professor," he said, flipping on his trusty cap. "Now—onward and upward shall we!"

XIII: The Forged Forgery

As we treaded carefully along the path I shuddered. "Quinby steered us true, von Stray with his rope idea. We owe him dearly. We would have fallen to our doom."

"I never doubted him, Dilpate. Still, I fear we may be too late to help Lady Elizabeth as a result of the delay. Undoubtedly the winds and heavy rains loosened the magnolia's hold on its petals."

As I looked down at the beach and saw large amounts of debris washed up along the shore, I knew von Stray was right. The magnolia would most likely be plucked clean. Although I didn't want to think it, we felt all along that Lady Elizabeth believed she would not live beyond the magnolia's flowering season; thus her insistence we locate the pearls in that time frame. I prayed that tree protected its own during the storm.

We doubled-timed it back to Gurnet Village arriving a little after 8:00 o'clock. Shop owners and villagers alike were busy inspecting their shops and cottages for storm damage. Already hammers were banging and saws buzzing. I looked out at the quaint harbor and all along the dock boat owners tugged and tightened their boat lines. At the far end of the dock a man was hunched over the stern, of a twenty-five foot runabout motor-boat and appeared to be fiddling with its engine. Meanwhile, a woman hidden under a lace umbrella and wearing a beautiful pink gown stood on the dock watching over the man's efforts. A small traveling bag and trunk rested at her feet.

As an avid sailor I saw a bit of humor in the man's engine trouble. "Look, von Stray...at the end of the dock. The sailboat isn't licked yet. If the man knew how to sail he and his female passenger could be enjoying a romantic voyage as we speak."

Von Stray glimpsed at them, and then turned away. "Indeed, Dilpate, but I see someone of greater interest—the village postal officer!"

"Good heavens, von Stray. What do we need with a postal officer? We must return to Suckling Manor at once."

"If the person who authored the mysterious poem lives locally, the village postal officer may recognize the author's handwriting?"

When we approached the postal officer, he was busy putting a push-broom to the storm debris strewn about the entrance of the general post office.

"Excuse me, sir," von Stray said, using his most disarming voice.

The postal officer halted his sweeping, leaned against his broom, and ran his eyes up and down us several times. "Pardon me gents, but you might want to tidy up a bit before your morning stroll. You look like you got dug up by a clumsy 'ound and dragged about the countryside."

I roiled. "Now see here, young man we're investigating a matter of the utmost—"

Von Stray cut in before I laid this chap out in lavender. "My name is Henry von Stray. I am a private detective from London and would be most appreciative if you could assist me with a very important case."

"Mr. Von Stray. I've 'eard of you from time to time in the newspaper columns. Name's Beccles. Pleased to make your acquaintance. This must be your man Dilpate."

I touched my hat rim. "Good morning, Beccles."

He looked at me cornerwise. "You're the professor. Beetles ain't it?"

"Yes, indeed. Thank you. In fact, I'm in the process of classifying a rare South American species—"

He cut me off. "Nasty things. 'Ow can I be of service, Mr. von Stray?"

"I would like to employ your expertise, Beccles."

He guffawed. "If I 'ad any expertise other than sortin' letters it would be all yours for the employin', mate."

Von Stray removed from his bag the object he'd carefully wrapped in oilskin and then uncovered the mysterious item. It was the vile poem left on Lady Elizabeth's writing desk. He handed it to Beccles. "That is precisely the expertise I wish to employ. Do you recognize this handwriting?"

Beccles filled his barrel chest with a bushel of sea air and exhaled. He then leaned his broom against the post office and took the poem from von Stray. He mumbled as he studied its handwriting. "Not that one…that one's good… no…good…good…no, no, no…and…another one n-n-no…not a chance on that one…wait…maybe…not bad…yes that one's quite all right…tsk, tsk, tsk…didn't even get a nibble on that one…this one though, I'd say quite all right indeed." He handed the document back to von Stray and shook his head. "It's a forgery, mate. Virtuoso who scribbled this rubbish better find 'imself another line of work less 'e got a 'ankering to spend some time in the nick."

Von Stray continued his inquiry. "Tell me, Beccles, are you able to tell us whose handwriting the author attempted to forge?"

Beccles snatched his broom off the wall and was overly cock-a-hoop with his analysis. "Can I tell! Course I can. I'm an expert on such important matters you know. Said so yourself. There isn't a letter that 'asn't passed through my 'ands and *very* watchful eye I might add in this village for the past *five* years or more. I could recognize anyone's 'andwriting 'ere in Gurnet with one 'and tied around my back. The bloke what scribbled that mess was trying to forge 'er Ladyship's beautiful 'and—Lady Elizabeth Victoria Thornbred, that is, to you outsiders."

I was mystified by the news. "Von Stray! The case grows more and more puzzling. Why would the culprit want to forge Lady Elizabeth's handwriting to make it appear as if she wrote this pernicious poem and then leave it on her desk?"

Von Stray rubbed his new wound before answering. "As I suspected, Dilpate, we are not confronted with a case of forgery—but rather one of disguise!"

"Good heavens, von Stray. Always in riddles. What do you mean 'disguise'?"

In his excitement my companion took a firm grip of my shoulder. "I will explain later, Dilpate. We haven't a moment to lose. I believe I now have enough information to give Ambrose that big push I promised you and solve the case. We must hurry back to Suckling Manor with all available dispatch."

As we sprinted down Suckling's crushed clamshell driveway, I observed the magnolia tree as we drew closer to the forecourt. "Look, von Stray. The storm obliterated the petals."

"I can see, Dilpate. We must hurry."

XIV: The Last of Derring-do Escapes

When we arrived at the manor house, senior footman Massey greeted us at the front-entrance door. He had a look of great relief at our safe return. "We were tremendously worried, gentlemen when you didn't return for dinner." He looked over our disheveled attire. "Er…shall I draw baths?"

Von Stray shook his head. "Thank you no, Massey. We will explain later, but first, we must see Her Ladyship at once."

Massey had a forlorn look about him. "Your suits would require a brushing before you could see Her Ladyship. Besides, I'm afraid you're too late, sir. Her Ladyship has departed."

"Good heavens!" I exclaimed. "Lady Elizabeth was right about the magnolia petals."

"Pardon me, sir. I mean Her Ladyship has left Suckling with Mr. Smethwick."

I looked at the great detective in complete bewilderment. "Von Stray, Lady Elizabeth has been abducted by that reprobate!"

A slight smile crossed von Stray's face as he questioned Massey. "Pray, when did they leave?

"I had their carriage ready at seven o'clock this morning, sir."

I suspected all along that there was something suspicious about Massey. "Had their carriage ready? You mean you aided and abetted this scoundrel Smethwick in his nefarious plot?"

Massey nodded politely. "I did indeed, sir."

I grew more and more outraged. "There, von Stray. He admits it. We must call the authorities post haste and make this conspirator tell us where they've hidden Lady Elizabeth. I bet he conspired to steal the pearls as well. Wait until a British jury gives him his just desert!"

Massey again nodded politely. "Correct again, sir." He addressed von Stray. "Her Ladyship is off to France with her…associate."

I was speechless.

Massey suddenly turned from us, and I was about grab him by the scruff of the neck before he got away when he calmly lifted a silver tray off a walnut table located in the foyer. He turned around and held the tray up to von Stray. On it rested a special dispatch from Sir Hamilton. "Perhaps this will explain matters, sir."

"Thank you, Massey," von Stray replied cordially. "You may return to your regular duties."

Massey offered a slight bow. "Thank you, sir."

"Von Stray! You're letting him escape? What about Her Ladyship? Not to mention the pearls?"

Von Stray opened the letter from Sir Hamiliton and read its contents silently. "As we suspected, Dilpate. Smethwick is not who he claims."

"What does Sir Hamilton have to say?"

Von Stray grinned as he handed me the note. I was absolutely dumfounded when I read the relevant portion of Sir Hamilton's May 7th report: "Edward Moreleans Smethwick born March 13, 1863 - died March 15, 1863."

"Von Stray! This confirms our suspicion that Smethwick is a fraud and plotted to take advantage of Her Ladyship. But…wouldn't she know the real Edward Smethwick died in infancy?"

"Indeed she would, Dilpate. I'm afraid we have been caught on the hop. Note the type of paper used by Sir Hamilton."

I inspected the document closely. "The threatening poem to Lady Elizabeth. Sir Hamilton uses the same type of paper! He is the fiend behind all of Lady Elizabeth's troubles. Obviously, he's contrived some monstrous plot to lay his greedy hands on the estate. We must inform the authorities at once."

"Hurry we must, Dilpate, but not to the authorities."

"Where then!"

"To the garden house if we expect to wish Her Ladyship a bon voyage!"

I followed my companion as he raced to the garden house where he climbed onto one of the push-bicycles and began pedaling pell-mell down the drive toward Gurnet Village. I pedaled with equal force behind him, and we reached the village dock in quicker time than it takes to tell.

The man at the end of the dock was still hunched over the motor-boat engine as we leaned our push-bicycles against an old gas lamppost located at the end of the boardwalk connecting to the dock. When the man looked up and saw us, he hurriedly made one final engine adjustment and then started the contraption. I nearly lost my footing when I saw it was the strange, black-bearded Bohemian man from the train. As we ran down the dock toward him, he gently guided his female guest aboard the small craft, hurled her luggage aboard, and then untied the docking lines. We were within a handful of yards from him when he leaped aboard the motor-boat making his escape as the craft drifted freely from the dock. Had we been a moment earlier we could have performed the same leap, but alas, the runabout had motored inches out of our reach.

As we stood at the end of the dock the man ripped off his beard and threw it into the air and laughed as it sailed into the harbor waters. He was the impersonator we knew only as Smethwick! The impersonator then picked something up from inside the boat and in a most amazing theatrical flourish tossed it into von Stray's artful hand. It was the impersonator's coveted walking stick.

In his great sonorous voice, the impersonator then recited over the harbor waters:

In God's name cheerly on,
courageous friends,
to reap the harvest of perpetual peace
by this one bloody trial of sharp war

When he finished, his female companion put her left arm through his right and in her own theatrical flourish threw a handful of magnolia petals into a calm sea breeze where they playfully danced in air before their inevitable fall onto the water's surface where they were instantly churned into the sea by the motor-boat's wake.

"Great Scott, von Stray! It's Lady Elizabeth!"

To my amazement von Stray gripped the walking stick's staff, brought its ivory handle to the brim of his trusty cap and saluted the voyagers. As they slipped further away from the dock, Lady Elizabeth blew him a kiss. For the first time I noticed the name of the boat painted in gold lettering on its stern: *Seasar's Pearls*.

"We must stop her, von Stray before she runs off for good with that… Bohemian lay-about!

"We will do nothing of the kind, Professor. Sir Morleans spent the first years of his life frolicking about the four corners of the earth. Why shouldn't Lady Elizabeth enjoy her few remaining days doing the same?"

As von Stray and I watched *Seasar's Pearls* disappear from the harbor my companion said, "A most magnificent woman, Dilpate. Magnificent indeed."

He then held out a hand. "Pray, my dear friend, may I borrow your spectacles?"

I exhaled. "Do be careful, von Stray."

He put on the spectacles and read aloud the inscription engraved into the walking stick's gold band: *To Barney McNulty, from his Providence, Rhode Island friends of Shakespeare, December 24, 1894.*

"Von Stray! Smethwick is really the great American stage actor Barney McNulty."

Von Stray leaned proudly into his new walking stick. "He is much more than that, Professor…he is Ariadne's long lost love Theseus! And to us, he is one of the many unsung heroes who helped put an end to the War."

"Good gad! Lady Elizabeth has fled with her American espionage contact from the War? Who will oversee Suckling Manor?"

A familiar voice startled us. "I will, Professor."

XV: Some Final Points

"Ambrose!" I exclaimed, unable to hide my joy in seeing my new friend in splendid form. We all shook hands and after extended greetings Ambrose said, reeling, "You both look like a haberdasher's nightmare. We must get you back to Suckling for a wringing and—" He cut himself short. "Von Stray, you've walloped your head!"

My companion pooh-poohed his injury. "All in the line of duty, Ambrose. We must trudge on together with the case."

Ambrose ran a hand over his head a few times. After a short pause he said, "Indeed, we must. Report in your findings, old man on the double."

Von Stray explained the circumstances surrounding Lady Elizabeth's departure.

Ambrose said, "So...Smethwick was really auntie's mate from the War, Barney McNulty. To tell you the truth, men, I always thought Smethwick was a bit off his bean. Never really believed he had Morleans blood in him."

"I quite agree," I said, using a silk handkerchief to polish the lenses of my spectacles. "I was suspicious of him all along."

Ambrose stared out at the harbor. "So Auntie's cut the apron strings. Good for her. I'm glad. Still, I'm afraid we're left with the impossible task of finding the missing pearls."

"To the contrary, Ambrose," insisted von Stray. "I can assure you that the clues you discovered in this most perplexing case have proved invaluable."

Ambrose looked astounded. "How, von Stray?"

"When we return to Suckling, I will show you just how your suppositions all but solve the riddle."

With dispatch we fastened the push-bicycles onto the boot of Ambrose's motor-car. On the return to Suckling he felt the need to explain how he happened upon us. "Pardon my own outfit, gents," he said, brushing sawdust off his overalls, "but a chum needed a hand knocking in a few loose boards after the storm. On the way back through the village I observed Suckling's push-bicycles propped against the lamppost and thought Catherine…well… found a new trail mate."

I hid my shock. First Lady Elizabeth and now Sir Ambrose. He was all but admitting he had fallen in love with a housemaid. The end of the War had brought about so many changes of this kind. Little by little, the old guard was loosening its grip on the working class. The England I knew was slipping away.

After arriving at Suckling, von Stray said to Ambrose, "We must return to where the pearls were last seen. It would be most helpful if you and Catherine would join us in Lady Elizabeth's quarters."

In Lady Elizabeth's bedroom von Stray thanked Catherine and Ambrose for their presence before knocking in the final pieces of the puzzle. "First, we must credit Sir Ambrose for his ingenious discovery that the man we now know as McNulty used a ladder to gain access to Lady Elizabeth's windows. Notwithstanding, I am convinced that McNulty did not steal the pearls but hid them."

I jumped in to straighten out my companion's analysis of the evidence. "But von Stray, we concluded that the ladder—"

My companion cut me off. "Exactly, Dilpate. That the ladder had been taken by McNulty from the garden house and used to carry out the deed."

I now understood von Stray's plan. He was carrying out Lady Elizabeth's directive to give Ambrose a little push in solving the case. I joined von Stray in the effort. "Yes, and thanks to your discovery, Ambrose, we were able to confirm that the ladder was indeed used by McNulty based on the fresh soil found on its butt ends as well as his tell-tale footprints."

Catherine put her right arm through Ambrose's left. "So very clever, Ambrose."

He blushed. "All a matter of logic, Catherine."

Von Stray ventured onward. "As I surmised a moment ago, I am convinced that McNulty took the pearls, not to steal them, but to hide them. After doing so he gave Lady Elizabeth a fortnight to make her decision whether or not to…voyage with him."

Recalling von Stray's lack of knowledge concerning botany, I explained the rather complicated scientific portion of his supposition. "Fourteen days of course is the approximate life expectancy of the magnolia's blossoming period and would explain why Lady Elizabeth invented this deadline to locate the pearls."

"Precisely, Dilpate." Von Stray then opened his leather bag and pulled out an envelope. He slid out from the envelope a soiled sheet of blotting paper. "I must apologize to you, Dilpate. The dropping of your spectacles into Lady Elizabeth's waste-bin was a simple ploy to obtain what I was really after. When I collected your spectacles, I also secreted out from the waste-bin this discarded sheet of blotting paper."

I didn't hide my bewilderment. "But when Catherine offered to empty the waste-bin Lady Elizabeth said she had created no rubbish in weeks."

Catherine shifted her stance. "Her Ladyship must have forgotten."

Von Stray shook his head. "I think not, Catherine, for the simple reason that her memory seemed quite clear when she informed us how she had remained in the habit of answering mail and forwarding notes to close friends. I thought it unusual that if she had been maintaining correspondence—then why would her blotter contain a fresh blotting sheet?"

"Yes, von Stray, the logical conclusion is now obvious. If a soiled blotting sheet had been replaced with a fresh one, the soiled one likely would find its way into her waste-bin."

"Exactly, Dilpate. Lady Elizabeth wanted me to find the soiled blotting sheet. I think we can all agree that a woman of her superior intelligence would not overlook this discrepancy. As a result, before taking my seat on the sofa I made a point of glancing into the waste-bin and my suspicions were at once confirmed when I observed the discarded blotting sheet. Hence, I created the subterfuge in order to rescue it from the incinerator."

I was agog. "Amazing, von Stray, but what can an old blotting sheet possibly tell us?"

Ambrose scratched his head. "Yes, what can we get out of that scrap? The blotted out letters are all higgledy-piggledy. You'd have better luck putting the magnolia petals back together."

Von Stray removed a small notepad and pencil he keeps in an inside pocket of his blazer and handed them to Catherine. "If my supposition is correct, I believe Catherine and I will be able to answer your question."

Catherine looked nonplussed. "Ambrose is right. The letters and words get all jumbled when squashed onto a blotting sheet. What possible help could I be?"

Von Stray removed a small mirror from his bag before answering. "I can assure you, Catherine that in a few moments you will be of great help indeed."

My companion then held his small mirror up to the soiled blotting sheet. "As you know when an author of a document uses a blotter to dry the wet ink of the words they have written onto a piece of paper, wet ink is transferred to the blotting sheet. The image of the words and letters, however, become reversed. If I hold the mirror next to the blotting sheet I recovered, we can look into the mirror and observe the letters in their proper form."

"This is fascinating, von Stray," I said, fighting back a yawn, "but I don't see what this could possibly tell us. I agree with Ambrose and Catherine, words and letters are scrambled all over the sheet. We'll never figure out what order the author intended."

Von Stray smiled. "With Catherine's help we soon will, Dilpate."

"How?" I pressed.

"Allow me to demonstrate. You will observe how even without using the mirror to reverse the image of the letters, that the sheet contains eleven uppercase letters. Catherine, please write them down in the order I give them to you as I hold the mirror to the sheet."

Von Stray read the letters out loud. When he was done, Catherine read off the following uppercase letters jotted down on the pad: S, T, E, C, K, N, A, D, E, L, N.

I remained bewildered. "This still gets us nowhere, von Stray. This isn't a word."

Ambrose paced. "Yes. I'm afraid Professor Dilpate is right."

Catherine interjected with great excitement. "But it is a word! It's the German word for 'pins.'"

"Exactly, Catherine," said von Stray, as he produced the morbid poem left on Lady Elizabeth's desk. He handed it to me, and I studied it carefully.

Say farewell, manor lass
To all you know
Each sun does pass
Closer reaps what you sow
Kindred spirits no more
No eyes folklore
All past is due
Death in the air
Everyone gone ado
Ladyship do despair
No pearls left to spare

"Ingenious! The uppercase letters from the blotting sheet are the first letters of each line and spell the German word for 'pins'. Good work, Catherine! Now if we can only figure out what the strange message means."

Von Stray said, "This blotting sheet all but confirms that the poem was written in this room by Her Ladyship. I submit the poem's author intended the word 'pins' to serve as the thread intended to lead us to the pearls' location. If we search this bedroom, I'm sure we'll discover where the thread leads us."

I wanted to help Ambrose but had little faith in von Stray's plan. "Von Stray, even though Catherine deciphered the mysterious poem, with Lady Elizabeth and McNulty gone we have no way of knowing how to decipher their final clue."

"Have faith, Dilpate. This is why I wanted both Catherine and Ambrose here. They know her habits better than anyone. Catherine, can you *point* to anything Lady Elizabeth might use regularly? Something McNulty would likely find in order to let him know she had discovered the hiding place?"

Catherine looked at von Stray intently. "Well...I can't quite *pinpoint*..."

Von Stray was persistent with his theory. "Keep in mind, Catherine and Ambrose that Lady Elizabeth and McNulty found cryptic ways to communicate during the War. We must think how and where she might have left him the secret message."

I sat down on the chesterfield next to Lady Elizabeth's famous sewing bag. I scooped up her pincushion and tossed it up in the air a couple of times while pondering how we might put our hands on the final clue. On my third toss Ambrose sprang in front of me and snatched the pincushion with lightening speed. "By gum, Professor, you are a genius. The pincushion! During the War Auntie would communicate her messages in Morse code to McNulty by the way she placed her flat pins. The final clue must be in the pincushion."

I shot up from the sofa. "Yes, of course, Ambrose. The pincushion must hold the remaining secret message."

We all huddled around the pincushion and examined the methodically arranged flat pins. Ambrose read off the order. "Let's see…three pins in a row that's a 'T' in Morse. Then one pin…small space…three in a row…small space…then one pin, that's an 'R'. Then one pin, that's an 'E'. Then one final pin, that's another 'E'."

The Morse code thus read: —, ●—●, ●, ●

"It spells 'TREE!'" I shouted.

"Masterfully done, Ambrose," von Stray congratulated. "You have discovered the hidden location of the pearls."

We rushed outside and Ambrose climbed the magnolia tree. With most of the pink petals gone the Sir Morleans pearls were easily spotted spliced between a few branch twigs. Ambrose gently unwrapped them from the tree's hold and they were safely back in the hands of their rightful owner. By this time Massey and Theodore were present to witness Ambrose recover his prized family legacy.

Ambrose climbed down from the tree and placed the pearls around Catherine's neck. "I knew I could solve the case."

Catherine beamed. "I never doubted you, Sir Ambrose." She turned and waved a hand over us. "*We* never doubted you."

With that she stood on the tips of her toes and kissed his cheek.

I couldn't have been more proud of this young woman who stood by her man in his hour of need. "To blazes with the old guard," I said to myself, then adding for good measure "and three cheers for the faithful housemaid—for *all* the housemaids!"

Von Stray put his arms around Massey and Theodore and we all instinctively shuffled into a huddle. Von Stray said, *sotto voce*, "Well, gentlemen, I think our business is complete here. Well done."

Theodore removed his beret: "For England, home, and beauty."

XVI: The Passenger Train to London

On the passenger train ride home to London I quizzed my companion. "Von Stray, I believe you knew all along this was an elaborate ruse masterminded by Lady Elizabeth."

"Not quite, Dilpate," he said, lighting his pipe. "Although, I became quite curious when Sir Hamilton informed us Her Ladyship insisted the pearls' return must occur before the magnolia dropped its petals. It is difficult to draw any logical connection between the two events. It's possible that a person in a weakened state might believe such an event is connected to their own mortality, notwithstanding, when I confirmed from Sir Hamilton, she was of sound mind, this possibility became even more remote."

"I see. She created the exigent deadline in order to hasten our investigative efforts in hopes it would expedite Ambrose's discovery."

He pulled on his pipe. "Partly, but I believe she had a practical reason as well. You must remember that the pearls are pink and as a result were camouflaged by the pink-colored petals. Once the petals dropped, the pearls would easily be spotted. In order for her ruse to work it was imperative that Sir Ambrose find the pearls and hence, not only receive credit for saving Suckling Manor, but making him feel worthy of Catherine."

"But why hide them in the tree and not some place else?"

"Why not? Because of her own poor health she knew the investigation could not go on indefinitely and, by having McNulty hide them in the tree she not only created the perfect pretext for the exigent time constraints, but could also keep a watchful eye on them. Not to mention a reliable ear on us as we investigated under her window. "

"But the ladder, von Stray," I said, continuing my interrogation, "we proved it was too short to reach her bay windows?"

"All part of the blind, Dilpate. McNulty placed the ladder under her window, climbed up as high as he could, and Her Ladyship simply dropped the pearls into his hand. He then climbed the tree and hid them where Ambrose found them. The deep depressions in the soil tend to confirm Ambrose's conclusion that someone did indeed climb the ladder."

"Amazing. Of course I knew all along something was suspicious about the convenient footprints. Smethwick…er…McNulty left a swath of clues wider than a King's highway."

Von Stray removed a small vile of honey from his bag and poured a generous dollop into his tea. As of late he has been visiting an older gentleman who has taken up beekeeping. "You have struck on the crux of the case, Dilpate. In Lady Elizabeth's bedroom, Catherine all but directed us to the wastebin. While a beautiful and honorable young woman of many talents, I'm afraid acting is not one of them."

"I quite agree. I suspected all along she was part of the ruse."

Von Stray continued. "Likewise, Lady Elizabeth's open sewing bag left on the sofa also seemed convenient. When I observed and read the pincushion's coded message, I suspected the pearls were in the tree. When I looked out the window, I saw them."

"Great Scott, von Stray! You knew where they were all along?"

He spread his hands. "Guilty. Notwithstanding, when Her Ladyship insisted we elicit Ambrose's assistance I quickly surmised her real objective was to have her nephew and sole heir regain his self-worth by allowing him to solve the mystery. Massey and Theodore not only were devoted to Lady Elizabeth, but as fellow veterans they were deeply concerned about Ambrose's well-being. They would do anything to help a fellow veteran including engaging in the extravagant ruse. All other attempts to help him had been unsuccessful, so what did they have to lose?"

I agreed without hesitation. "Naturally you and I would do the same for a fellow veteran if we had the chance. Von Stray, there is one other mystery which requires explanation. Who forged the poem in Lady Elizabeth's handwriting?"

He picked up a spoon and stirred his tea. "No one, Professor. When I left you and Ambrose in his study to decipher the poem's clue, I put my mirror test to the blotting sheet and when I discovered the German word for 'pins', this confirmed beyond mere speculation that the poem had been written in Lady Elizabeth's bedroom. Later, our new friend from the post office—Beccles—concluded that someone tried to forge Lady Elizabeth's handwriting. I submit it wasn't a forgery attempt, but rather an attempt by Lady Elizabeth to disguise her own handwriting."

I nodded. "Ahh…a brilliant red herring…of course…"

He sipped tea. "Quite. The poem and discarded blotting sheet were designed to complicate her ingenious blind. The more red herrings—the more rewarding it would be for Ambrose to unravel the mysterious affair."

"Quite clever, yet it's still unclear to me why Lady Elizabeth did not take us into her confidence."

Von Stray raised the new walking stick he received from McNulty. "You are forgetting the second prong of her plan, Professor. Lady Elizabeth's alter ego 'Ariadne' wished to free herself of Suckling's bonds and spend her final days in peace with her kindred spirit 'Theseus.' Incidentally, her voyage should not be construed as an act of self-indulgence, but a final act of love and devotion to Sir Ambrose."

"How so?" I asked

"I fear, Professor that her days are indeed few. Her Ladyship's departure from Suckling with her feet still firmly on the ground—or should I say firmly on *Seasar's Pearls*—was a vote of complete confidence in Sir Ambrose's ability to manage the estate's affairs. The divulgence of the plan would have required revealing Smethwick's true identity. This would further the risk of disclosing their secret plan to engage in one final adventure. All Ariadne required of us was to stitch the clues together for Sir Ambrose to follow. Other than McNulty, Sir Hamilton is likely the only other person who knew of her entire plan."

"Goodness gracious, von Stray! You don't mean to say Sir Hamilton was privy to the whole scheme?"

"Undoubtedly," he said, reaching for his pipe. "As the family's long-time legal advisor, it is not credible that a barrister of his intellect would be unaware of Edward Smethwick's short stay on earth, and therefore, McNulty's role as the disgruntled cousin. Further, Sir Hamiliton's missive regarding Edward's death was dated Wednesday—the day *before* he met with us in London. He anticipated I would ask him to investigate Smethwick, and had the information at the ready all along. At the appropriate time, Lady Elizabeth forwarded the note to us through Massey."

"Amazing, von Stray. Do you think the whole desperate enterprise will really help Ambrose recover?"

Von Stray bit on the end of his pipe before lighting it. He sat for a moment in deep reflection. "I must believe…we *all* must believe a little push motivated by motherly love will ultimately generate more force than a big push orchestrated by tyrants, but I venture to guess our new friend still has a long road ahead."

I looked out the train's window and saw von Stray's battle scar and fresh wound reflecting off the glass. As a thin veil of pipe smoke drifted lazily over his face, I thought how the invisible scars of war would never disappear without a good fight, we were all just holding the line. A line my dear friend and I rarely talked about, yet instinctively knew our duty to hold it together. "I guess we're all on that same road, von Stray, but now Ambrose has a strong woman to guide him. Speaking of which, how the devil did you know Catherine understood German?"

Von Stray looked up pleasantly. "For this, Dilpate we must credit your discriminating palate. I doubt there is another Englishman alive who could recognize an authentic German bee sting cake with more efficiency than yourself."

I pulled on my moustache and held an inquiring gaze upon my friend. He looked back at me and at once we burst into thunderous laughter. So thunderous it nearly toppled our carriage off the tracks and into the English countryside.

Epilogue: Last of the Lost Pearls

In the weeks following the events at Suckling Manor, von Stray found refuge in his kitchen as he often does when not up to snuff. He went on a cooking spree baking enough soda breads, brown breads, and plum breads to feed the Berkeley Street Orphanage for Girls. To this day it remains a mystery to me as to what he did with those mountainous piles of delicious-smelling breads.

Then one afternoon while we were enjoying tea and some of von Stray's extraordinary rhubarb jam lathered on homemade Scottish oatcakes, a letter addressed to "Mr. Henry von Stray" arrived. When my dear companion announced the letter bore a Gurnet Village post-mark, and was addressed from Lady Catherine Moreleans of Suckling Manor, his spirits boosted immediately. While in the comfort of our respective easy chairs he read aloud the letter's contents:

Dear Mr. von Stray,

Our note of appreciation is overdue. You must forgive me as Ambrose and I have only recently returned from our honeymoon. We had a glorious time in the Riviera where we spent a great deal of time entertained by a most charming elderly couple who insisted on taking us to the theater each evening. We shall miss them terribly as they do not foresee visiting England anytime in the near future. Our own travel will also be on hold as Ambrose, with the help of Norman and Theodore, is busy refurbishing the old stable. He is converting it into a home and trade school for veterans. Norman and Theodore have agreed to stay on as trade instructors. Ambrose says that with taxes the way they are after the War the stable hasn't seen a horse in a dog's age anyway, so it's no sacrifice. Is it wrong that I secretly take delight in his tax complaints? The project has been a wonderful distraction for Ambrose and as a result his sudden jaunts are less frequent. You will be happy to know that Suckling and the new school are on sound financial footing. Sir Hamilton fixed it so we could sell the Sir Morleans Pearls for a vast sum of money without violating the family trust or death duties. Some complicated legal gift-scheme among the living. Please give my kindest regards to Professor Dilpate. Ambrose and I, and all the future students of the school, will be forever indebted to the Professor for his most ingenious discovery of the pincushion's code. Incidentally, the small oak tree Professor Dilpate asked Theodore to transplant is thriving here at Suckling and Ambrose is keeping meticulous records of its progress.

In everlasting friendship, I am,

Most lovingly yours,

Lady Catherine Morleans

P.S. Ambrose has named the school: The Vocational School for Morleans' Pearls.

After reading the letter von Stray returned it to its envelope and placed it carefully into his breast pocket. "A gift-scheme among the living! Why, with Lady Elizabeth's own disappearance she and Suckling's Vocational School can go on living forever. Brilliant! A magnificent woman indeed, Dilpate!"

"Von Stray!" I roared. "They've sold the pearls. They were the family's most important legacy."

"I think not, Dilpate when you consider the pearls they get in return. A fair rate of exchange at any price."

After pondering my friend's words, I stood up, raised my cup of tea, and said, "My dear friend, please join me in a toast: For Mankind, home and beauty! May the War to end all wars truly be the last of the lost pearls."

II

The Case of the Illustrious Banker

John McAleer

From the Desk of
Professor John W. Dilpate
Berkeley Square, London
4 August 1925

The Case of the Illustrious Banker

If it weren't for my dear friend Mr. Henry von Stray, Inspector Bernard Renyalds would undoubtedly still be gnawing on soda biscuits in his Scotland Yard office while pondering the strange and baffling events behind the Derrycastle murder.

It was a bright and crisp spring morning when I entered the sitting room of the tidy flat I share with von Stray at No. 121B Berkeley Street, London. I was on sabbatical from the University Clifford and had just completed a brisk early walk through the public garden only to find myself stepping into thick aromatic clouds of pipe smoke. The great private detective, Henry von Stray, sat ensconced in his favorite parlour easy chair, his London briar pipe at full steam. He was reading the latest edition of the *London Star*. After removing my khaki blazer and flat cap, I slid into my easy chair opposite him near a set of windows overlooking the morning throng of industrious Londoners.

Von Stray greeted me without lifting his eyes from the newspaper. "And how is my dearest friend and able colleague, Professor John W. Dilpate, on this refreshing April morning?"

I patted the sides of my stomach and said to my companion, "I seem to recall something about a hearty breakfast?"

"Breakfast?"

"Indeed, von Stray. Let me refresh your memory: pots of hot coffee, boiled eggs, sausage, hot cakes, crumpets, strawberry-rhubarb jam, and cheese. Oh, and some of that delicious honey you manage to procure from that retired chap you consult at irregular intervals. We're growing boys, you know?"

"My dear Dilpate, you'll lose that slight frame of yours if you continue to partake in such feasts," said von Stray, in his jovial voice.

I looked at von Stray over the tops of my gold-rimmed spectacles. I paused for a moment as I was still getting used to my companion's clean-shaven face. Exigent circumstances necessitated his moustache's removal during the singularly strange case of the Murder at Lord Beachy's. "Codswallop!" I protested. "I don't carry a half-stone more than I did during my boxing days with the Royal Navy—and I dare say any addition is the result of muscle tone. My brisk walks and regular Indian club exercise regimens see to that."

I began a short lecture on the fascinating modern science behind Indian club physical fitness training methods, such as the poise-and-drop, inward sweeps, and shoulder braces, but it was no use trying to engage the great criminologist von Stray on this exciting subject. Whatever held his attention in the *Star* had put an abrupt end to our breakfast plans. It wouldn't be the first time.

He folded the newspaper neatly and said to me, "Did you see this item in the *Star* about the bewildering death of D. P. Derrycastle of the London Trust Company?"

I waved my hand through a thick fog of Prince Albert tobacco smoke and adjusted my seating position to avoid the exhaust bursting from Von Stray's pipe. "Not the same D. P. Derrycastle accused of swindling A. F. Scott back in 1911?"

Von Stray lightly rubbed the small scar located on the upper left side of his forehead. A small "memento" as he calls it from his service in the trenches during the war. "Precisely. I've always had a feeling that Scott really was swindled. But as you may recall, Dilpate, his case was thrown out of court. He died in less than six months, leaving a wife and child. His wife evidently could not bear the humiliation and disgrace, for she disappeared shortly afterwards and has not been heard of since."

"Yes," I said, "a nasty affair."

"No doubt a black eye to the justice system," said von Stray, knocking out his pipe into the ruffled clam-shell ashtray he kept on top of an end table he constructed from Massaranduba wood imported from Brazil. "But now let's get back to the present Derrycastle matter. I suppose you will be interested to know how he met his unfortunate death?"

I nodded and von Stray read the following item from the *Star*:

Noted Banker Dead! Police Suspect Foul Play!

London—As Mr D. P. Derrycastle, President of the London Trust Company, entered his office yesterday morning, he stopped in his outer office to tell his secretary, Miss Ethel Kirby, to come into his private office at 9.15 a.m. to take a letter he would dictate to her. It was then 9.00 a.m.

At 9.05 a.m., Mr Samuel Gogan entered Derrycastle's office to talk over some business with him. He left a few minutes later. When Miss Kirby entered Derrycastle's office to take the letter at 9.15 a.m., she did not see him in the office. She thought he had gone into the vice president's office by the private door connecting the two rooms, so she sat down to wait for him to return.

After she had been waiting a few minutes, she became impatient and decided to investigate. As she started to rise from her chair, she noticed a foot protruding from behind Derrycastle's large desk. Upon investigating, she found—much to her horror and dismay!—Derrycastle's body lying on the floor behind the desk. She summoned the clerks located in the bank's outer office, and they quickly sent for a doctor.

A local doctor, Nigel Kenyard, arrived on the scene and determined that Derrycastle had been electrocuted. He said the police had better be summoned, as it looked as if Derrycastle had been murdered.

The police have detained Gogan as a suspicious party, but, as of yet, have not arrested him for killing Derrycastle. The guilty party appears to have left no clues.

Inspector Bernard Renyalds of Scotland Yard admits frankly that this is the most baffling case since the affair of the Westminster Miser. Inspector Renyalds added that it was a mystery as to how Derrycastle was electrocuted as his office had not been updated with electricity.

Miss Kirby was held for questioning, but later released. She is now resting in her home at 2½ Denton Street, suffering from nervous strain due to the strenuous ordeal she has undergone in the last 24 hours. Miss Kirby came to London from Blackpool five years ago and has been Derrycastle's secretary for two years.

Von Stray laid down the paper, "I am quite confident that our very dear friend, Inspector Renyalds, will ask my help in solving this curious affair, as he has done in many of his former cases."

"Ah, yes," I said, rubbing my moustache and noting that it was in desperate need of a trim and waxing. "It seems to me he rarely solves a case without our help. Take the case of the Westminster Miser, for example. I am willing to wager five pounds he'll be here within an hour."

Scarcely had my words been spoken when we heard the sharp ringing of the doorbell.

I swung my head in the direction of the front entrance. "Who the deuce could that be calling at this hour of the morning?"

Von Stray moved to the edge of his seat, his pipe canted in his left hand. "Pray answer the door, Dilpate, my good fellow. I believe that is the inspector now."

I opened the door and in stepped a tall, dark-complexioned man approximately forty years old sporting a thick, red moustache—Inspector Renyalds himself. He was rather plump, but with a muscular build through the shoulders, and his barrel chest.

"Good morning, Professor," rumbled the inspector in his stentorian voice. "Is Mr von Stray available?"

"Indeed I am, Inspector," said von Stray, rising with enthusiasm. "I was expecting you. No doubt you are here to obtain my assistance in the Derrycastle case."

"How did you know?" said Renyalds, removing his derby hat.

"You have asked for my help with all other important cases you have been connected with for the past several years," said von Stray.

"I am quite sure you do not know all the facts of the Derrycastle case," said the inspector, lifting his blocky chin a notch. "We have been fortunate enough to keep our latest discoveries out of the paper."

"Perhaps," said von Stray, waving his hand over my easy chair inviting Renyalds to sit, "even greater fortune will shine upon you by acquainting us with all the known facts to date."

Inspector Renyalds found his way to my easy chair and began to fill us in on the remarkable events. Before he started, my companion stepped away from his chair and paced the room. His hands were clasped behind his back and his pipe clenched between his teeth. As he paced, I glanced at the portrait of his great-grandfather Captain Frederick von Stray that hangs above the sitting room fireplace. He served as a distinguished Danish infantry officer in the previous century. I often think the dearly departed Captain—his keen grey eyes on constant lookout—takes as much interest in von Stray's adventures as I do. I then cleared myself from the decks and glided into von Stray's vacated seat.

"Very well then," began the inspector, rubbing his square jaw with a hand the size of a ham. "Upon questioning Miss Kirby, we found that Derrycastle and Gogan were engaged in a bitter argument during their conversation a short time before Derrycastle's mysterious death. Since we discovered this interesting fact, we have questioned Gogan. At first he denied the charges, but after putting him under considerable pressure, we finally got him to admit that he had a heated discussion with Derrycastle during his meeting with him. But he still insists that it was a mere disagreement over a business matter and has no bearing on the case whatever. He's gone through quite a grilling and still won't break down and confess to the crime. Tough as auntie's mutton he is. Now I am not quite sure that he is guilty."

"Why, Inspector?" I enquired. "It seems plain as a pikestaff. No one else was present to commit the ghastly deed. Unless of course the bank's vice president is responsible?"

The inspector shook his head. "The vice president's door adjoining Derrycastle's office was deadbolted from Derrycastle's side. Besides, he was out on business. Anyway, the vice president couldn't have entered without Derrycastle himself opening the door and then locking it again from his side. The only other passage is through Miss Kirby's outer office, and she insisted none of the clerks or vice president entered through her office. No one gets in or out without passing her."

Von Stray said, "And you credit Miss Kirby's statement on this point as well as the vice president's alibi, Inspector?"

"I regret to say that I do. I say 'regret' because their statements only add to the puzzle. We haven't found any motive other than Gogan's argument with the victim."

Von Stray asked, refilling his pipe with deliberate care, "Are there any windows in Derrycastle's office?"

Renyalds shook his head. "None. This fact only adds to my worries, so I've come here to ask for your help, von Stray. Will you be kind enough to contribute your invaluable time and assistance to this case by doing a little investigation on the side? Lest, I'm ashamed to admit, we might possibly be on the wrong trail—though I don't see how."

"I surely will," said von Stray, lightly massaging his scar. "Always have time for others and others will have time for you. Besides, you don't know how this case interests me."

In his excitement, Renyalds nearly crushed his derby with his huge hands. "Sterling, von Stray! Sterling! You may question any of the people connected with the murder, and you can visit the crime scene as often as you like. I only hope that you and Professor Dilpate will find some clues."

Von Stray plucked a match from his Royal Doulton "Old Salty" mug, struck it against the brick fireplace, and lit his pipe. The burning tobacco filled the room with subtle notes of cocoa and molasses. He said, through puffs of tobacco smoke, "If my usual luck keeps up, as it has since my crime-solving career started, I think we will."

"Well," said the inspector, "I will have to make my visit brief as there are several smaller details to attend to." Renyalds pulled a wrinkled envelope out of his hat and handed it to me. "Speaking of details, here's a small letter of introduction I prepared in case you need it during the course of your investigation—Yard stationery and all."

I accepted the envelope and nodded. "Indeed! Thank you, Inspector. Quite official."

Von Stray removed his pipe long enough to ask, "Oh, by the way, Inspector, have you found out for certain if Derrycastle did in fact die by means of electrocution?"

"Most certain," confirmed the inspector. "The police surgeon's postmortem has reached the same conclusion as Dr Kenyard. Derrycastle's hands were terribly burned from what appears to be some kind of strong electric current. A nippy bit of work indeed."

I put my spectacles up. "Impossible. According to the *Star* you said Derrycastle's office had no electricity!"

Von Stray whisked his pipe stem from his mouth. "Careful, Professor. According to the *Star* report the inspector merely stated that the office had not been *updated* with electricity."

"That's true, von Stray," Renyalds said, pulling on his reddish moustache. "But I agree with the professor. I don't see the difference."

I turned an inquiring gaze on my companion. "Yes, neither do I?"

"Perhaps it's a small matter," von Stray conceded. "Just one more question, Inspector. Did Gogan say what his disagreement with Derrycastle concerned?"

The inspector showed the palm of his right hand. "Turns out Gogan is one of those crack-pot inventor types. Claims the bank refused to underwrite his latest contraption—a radio with pictures." The inspector snickered, "Tommyrot."

Here I observed the familiar bright twinkle fill my companion's left eye. He then walked over to Renyalds and gave him a firm handshake. "Thank you and good day, Inspector. I hope to have some *sterling* news for you when I see you next!"

With a further exchange of compliments Inspector Renyalds parted.

* * *

After the inspector left, we breakfasted quickly. During breakfast von Stray skimmed through one of his scrapbooks from his voluminous collection of newspaper articles and other odds and ends. I was just about to excuse myself to groom my moustache when he said, "Dilpate, my good fellow, I think our friend the inspector is on the wrong trail, so hurry now and put on your coat and fetch your umbrella. We are going to do some real investigating."

My companion fetched his ivory-handled walking stick presented to him by the great American stage actor Barney McNulty who found himself peripherally entangled in "The Case of Sir Morelans' Lost Pearls."

"Where to?" I asked.

"To where the trail first leads us, my dear professor. Where else!" von Stray said, flipping on his ancient, wool-tweed cap.

"Always in riddles," I said, wrestling my way into my coat, "always in riddles. Umbrella! There's not a cloud in the sky. And what about my moustache?"

Von Stray, already halfway out the front door, shouted, "By all means take it with you if you must."

* * *

Von Stray hailed a cab after we left the apartment and instructed the driver to take us to the residence of Miss Kirby at No. 2½ Denton Street. This proved to be a large apartment house under the name of Denton Chambers. We had little trouble locating Miss Kirby's apartment, and five minutes later we were comfortably seated on a large Victorian divan in her parlour.

Miss Kirby was a comely and dignified woman of about three-and-twenty. Upon questioning Miss Kirby, von Stray found that her story was the same as the one she had told the police.

At the conclusion of her account, von Stray pointed to a nearby table. I noted the familiar bright twinkle in his left eye as the great detective said to Miss Kirby, "I couldn't help noticing the photograph of the beautiful woman beside you, Miss Kirby."

The photograph my colleague referred to was encased in a small, ornate, gold-tone frame and rested on the walnut end table convenient to Miss Kirby. Next to the photograph sat a porcelain vase holding a fresh, single white lily.

Miss Kirby became of a crimson colour just before picking up the photograph. "Well…er…this was my dear cousin." She then casually returned the photograph to the table facing it away from our view. A hint of sadness filled her blue eyes. No doubt this poor, innocent young lady still suffered from shock.

"My apologies, Miss Kirby. I thought I noted a family resemblance, but I didn't mean to intrude into your personal matters."

"Oh, think nothing of it, Mr von Stray," said Miss Kirby as a shy smile played about her lips. "I will be only too glad to assist you in any way I can, so that this ghastly affair can be solved and the guilty party brought to justice."

Von Stray nodded politely and rose from the divan. "We must be going, and I assure you, Miss Kirby, you will soon realize what a help you have been to us."

After bidding Miss Kirby a cordial good day, we departed.

* * *

As we made our way through the crowded streets of London, a drizzly bit of rain greeted the city. I opened my umbrella (which I had the good sense and foresight to bring) and then we continued on our way, each of us no doubt analysing what we had learned from Miss Kirby. There could be no question about it in my mind. With Miss Kirby confirming her account of the events and the vice president's unshakable alibi confirmed by Scotland Yard, the only possible culprit left was Gogan.

I was about to share my conclusions with von Stray when he stopped before a telegraph office on Regent Street and said, "Dilpate, wait here a minute." He disappeared into the telegraph agency while I took some additional cover under the awning of an ancient Piccadilly peanut vendor.

Big Ben was chiming the quarter after one when the vendor cast an eye at me cornerwise and said despondently, "Sorry for your troubles, guv."

"Er…troubles?" I enquired, while selecting a bag of roasted peanuts.

He appeared even further crestfallen now. "Pardon me, guv, but your moustache is in a frightful flap with the rest'a your face. She must 'a broke your poor wee 'eart I bet that ol' she devil did."

"See here, old man—" I began, ready to lay the old bloke out in lavender, but my verbal walloping was cut short when von Stray popped out of the telegraph office. I paid for my peanuts and left the vendor abruptly.

My companion and I walked back to our digs, where we settled into our respective easy chairs to ponder the baffling problems before us. At first opportunity, however, I excused myself and put order to my untidy moustache. I always think better when properly groomed.

When I returned, a bag of peanuts had found their way into my possession. I also found von Stray in deep contemplation, absently massaging his memento. I knew better than to disturb my friend's solitude, so I refrained from asking him questions about his strange visit to the telegraph office. I had just cracked the last peanut shell when von Stray announced, after what seemed like an eternal silence, "Dilpate, I've despatched a telegram to Blackpool and expect an answer at any time. While waiting, what would you say to dinner at the Barrymore Club?"

I quickly crumpled up my empty peanut bag and lobbed it into the fireplace. "Excellent suggestion. I always think better on a bit of English fare. If memory serves me correctly Miss Alcorn's famous pigeon pie and pickled salmon headline the menu this evening."

* * *

After partaking of a light, but nourishing meal at the Barrymore Club with our good friend from the Fraternal Order of Benevolent Walnuts, Sir Percy Stonyhurst Berrycloth, we returned to our humble retreat. My companion rummaged through his files and scrapbooks for the remainder of the evening. I spent the time classifying some rare beetle specimens, which the noted Professor Ambrose Leanaou of Harvard University had sent me from South America. Little did I realize, as I pondered my prized collection of insects, that von Stray was making some most interesting discoveries in the brief time we had been on the Derrycastle case. At 11.30 p.m. we deemed it advisable to retire.

* * *

I am an early bird. At 8.00 a.m. next morning, after conducting my Indian club exercise regimen in the public garden, I found von Stray seated at the dining table with a delightful spread consisting of deviled sole, homemade raisin scones, boiled eggs, butter, quince jam, honey, and piping hot coffee. Von Stray became an excellent cook after the war.

On the breakfast table, a small envelope from the telegraph agency sat beneath a walrus tusk honed into a letter opener. My companion was massaging his scar as he usually does when engaging in deep analytical thought. From this I deduced he'd received some important reply from the previous day's telegraph inquiry. A morning edition of the *London Star* was also on the table. I adjusted my spectacles and could make out from the headlines that the *Star* was openly accusing Scotland Yard of being baffled with the Derrycastle murder.

I cleared my throat and sat down. "Not that it is any of my business, von Stray, but I would like to know what this telegram business is all about. I thought you would soon tell me, but as you have still advanced no explanation, I'll take it upon myself to ask."

"You know curiosity killed the cat, my dear Dilpate." Von Stray poured me a cup of piping hot coffee. "I am going to keep you in suspense a little while longer. Then it will surprise you all the more. However, I will venture so far as to say that the crime will be solved within twenty-four hours."

"By Jehoshaphat, von Stray," said I, reaching for one of his warm scones, "your ability to make bricks without straw never ceases to amaze me."

Von Stray smiled as he reached for his jar of honey. "Correction, my learned friend. It's the honey, not the straw that forms my bricks. Remember, 'He who eats honey, thinks honey.' Furthermore," he continued, after helping himself to a generous spoonful of honey, "poor Gogan is an innocent man and will be completely exonerated from any connection with this crime."

I lathered a scone with butter and quince jam. "You're talking in riddles as far as I'm concerned. But lead on, von Stray."

"If I am able to obtain the direct evidence I need, my supposition will be watertight," he said, rising to clear his dishes. "And I hope to find that direct evidence this morning."

I sprang up from the table, nearly spilling my coffee. "When do we start! If we've cleared Gogan, the trail can only lead to this Dr Kenyard. I'd bet my last shilling he deliberately bungled the facts of the case in order to draw the authorities off the scent. Claiming that Derrycastle's death was caused by electric shock—fiddle-faddle! I bet that old parsimonious blighter Derrycastle was poisoned somehow."

"You're getting ahead of yourself, old man," said von Stray, now snatching up a battered leather bag he carries for search purposes. "But the inspector is right that this is a nippy bit of work indeed. Every second we waste, an innocent man rots behind bars. Let's not make the same obvious mistakes the authorities have. As I have said many times, 'Cases resting solely on circumstantial evidence tend to invite false inferences.'"

* * *

Von Stray and I visited the London Trust situated at the corner of Pell Street and Firling Avenue to examine the scene of the murder. As we approached the bank, a brisk, ruddy-faced police constable ordered us to an abrupt halt. We recognized him at once as our good friend, Constable Vincent Hastings. Since I have been recording the exploits of von Stray and his unique analytic methods of crime detection, I have taken particular note of how von Stray's war memento (and I might add my own service in the Royal Navy) have given us considerable sway with other civil servants who served in the big scrap. We had also assisted Hastings with a little problem involving a beautiful Italian acrobat a while back, so I knew he would be delighted to see us on the job.

"Ah, Hastings, old chap," von Stray said, presenting our credentials from Inspector Renyalds providing us with authorization to enter the crime scene.

"No need for a bushel of nipperty-tipperty paperwork, Mr von Stray," said Hastings, waving away the document with a gentle wag of his nightstick. "You're one of us blokes." He then pointed his nightstick in my direction. "Who's this chap again…?"

Von Stray responded. "This is my colleague Professor Dilpate as you may recall."

"Oh…right. Okay, 'e can enter as long as 'e's with you, Sir," Hastings said, producing a pass-key to unlock the bank's front door.

I was just about to enter the bank when Hastings lowered his nightstick in front of me like a railroad crossing gate. "'Old your 'orses there, mate, 'ave to turn off the bank alarm system. Complicated bit 'a machinery it is."

Just over the threshold of the London Trust entrance, Hastings switched on the electric lights. He then opened a small alarm box containing a maze of wires and contraptions, pulled out a special key, fit it into the box and turned the key to disengage the alarm system. Needless to say, I was fascinated by the complexity of the alarm system and Hastings skill in disengaging it so efficiently.

"All set, gents." Hastings touched his helmet rim and left us to examine the crime scene.

Von Stray instructed me to look through Miss Kirby's desk and office, while he entered Derrycastle's private office. Her office consisted of a standard secretary's desk, gas lamps, an old No. 10 Remington typewriter, water-cooler, a couple of oak filing cabinets, and, among a few other unimportant items, a wastepaper basket.

Twenty minutes had elapsed when von Stray emerged and enquired if I had found anything of interest. I replied that I found nothing, save some crumpled sheets of paper in the wastepaper basket with some bits of wires and old tools underneath.

"It struck me as a rather odd place to dispose of them," I said.

"Ah!" said von Stray with an air of delight. "That is just what I anticipated." He then opened several of the crumpled papers and examined them. "Just what I suspected, Dilpate. These sheets are blank."

"More riddles, von Stray?" I said, rubbing my chin.

"I believe, Dilpate, that our investigation is near complete." Von Stray then swept the wires and tools into his leather bag. "First, come with me. I'd like to check a couple of more items with you present."

I followed von Stray into Derrycastle's office. Von Stray turned up a gas lamp, but the windowless office remained a bit dim. It was an austere setting consisting of a few oak filing cabinets, large mahogany desk, humidor, large ashtray, pen and ink, and, among other unimportant items, a candlestick telephone. My companion removed a small electric torch from his leather bag. After turning it on he held its beam of light against the deadbolt locking mechanism located on the door connecting to the vice president's office.

After examining it for a moment he held out a hand in my direction. "Pray, Dilpate, may I borrow your spectacles?"

I took them off reluctantly and handed them to him. "I don't know why you don't keep a magnifying glass in that bag of tricks you carry. You're always borrowing my spectacles on these occasions."

Von Stray put them on and examined the deadbolt more closely. "Why use one magnifying glass when I can examine the evidence through both eyes belonging to my able collaborator in the detection of crime!"

I showed remarkable restraint. "Well…please don't twist up the frames like you have a tendency to do."

After examining the deadbolt for what seemed an extended period, he pulled off my spectacles as if he were pulling a string of yarn and then handed them back to me. "Here, Dilpate, take a look."

I straightened out the delicate spectacle frames and put them back on. I then stooped down to examine the area in question. "I don't see anything, von Stray. No fresh scuff or scratch marks on the locking mechanism." I twisted the deadbolt back and forth a few times. "It's in perfect working order."

"Precisely. As you can see there are no fresh signs of tampering. This independently corroborates Miss Kirby's statement to Scotland Yard that no one could enter Derrycastle's office from the vice president's office without someone unbolting the lock from Derrycastle's side. With this type of deadbolt, it logically follows that it must be re-bolted from Derrycastle's side as Inspector Renyalds found it had been."

"I quite agree," I said to my companion. "Of course, I never doubted Miss Kirby. A fine, respectable, young woman of great intelligence."

Von Stray said without check, "Yes, old chap… A woman of superior intelligence indeed."

He then walked over to Derrycastle's desk and began examining the candlestick telephone. Anticipating his next move I handed him my spectacles. When he was through with his examination, he said, whisking off my spectacles, "By Jove, Dilpate! Just as I suspected. Upon closer examination these are undoubtedly fresh markings around the telephone's wiring connections."

While repairing my frames, I enquired, "Marks and no marks, what does it all mean, von Stray?"

"It means we're off to Scotland Yard to report our findings!"

* * *

We hailed a cab, and in less time than it takes to tell, we were seated in the comfortable New Scotland Yard office of Inspector Renyalds on Victoria Embankment overlooking the River Thames.

"Inspector," said von Stray, "I believe that I've found a solution to this terrible crime. Direct your men to arrest Derrycastle's secretary, Miss Kirby."

"What!" said the inspector, rising with a start from his chair and nearly sending it swiveling into the Thames.

Von Stray repeated calmly, "Arrest Miss Kirby."

Even I was taken aback by von Stray's words.

"Why, that's impossible," said the inspector.

"Not quite," said von Stray as he filled his briar pipe. "However, to set your mind at ease, I'll tell you what our investigations have disclosed."

"Very well." Renyalds scooped a soda biscuit out from a side pocket of his houndstooth jacket. "Get on with it."

"A baffling affair," explained the great detective. "Professor Dilpate and I decided to pay Miss Kirby a visit and question her concerning the murder. While there, I chanced to see a photograph resting on a nearby table. I immediately noticed that Miss Kirby bore a remarkable resemblance to the woman in the photograph. I simply asked Miss Kirby the identity of the woman, but she replied nervously 'a dear cousin.' Then she picked up the photograph and returned it facing away from my line of vision.

"This aroused my curiosity, for I had a vague memory of seeing that photograph somewhere before. Suddenly, it came to me that the lady in the photograph was the wife of A. F. Scott who, you remember, claimed some fourteen years ago that he was swindled by Derrycastle."

Renyalds bit into his biscuit and chewed rapidly. "Yes, go on."

"As you already know," von Stray continued, "Miss Kirby claims she was born in Blackpool. I had my suspicions, so I despatched a telegram to the registry of births at Blackpool, inquiring if a Miss Eunice Kirby was born there. I received a negative answer this morning. This confirmed my suspicions that Miss Kirby is, in reality, A. F. Scott's daughter. I knew then that she was the one who killed Derrycastle to avenge her father's disgrace and untimely death. I needed more proof, however.

"Therefore, I visited the scene of the crime with my invaluable coadjutor, Professor Dilpate, and while he searched Miss Kirby's outer office, I did a little investigating of my own in Derrycastle's private office. There I found that the wires to his candlestick telephone had been tampered with recently. I further confirmed this with Professor Dilpate as witness."

I nodded. "Yes…completely confirmed—you can bank on it, Inspector."

Von Stray proceeded. "I immediately realized that someone—no doubt Miss Kirby—had created an electronic connection in such a manner that whoever touched the metal receiver and metal stem of the telephone would be electrocuted. While the bank's offices had not been updated with electricity, the main lobby of the bank had. Moreover, the bank was equipped with an intricate electrical alarm system. A system undoubtedly tapped into by Miss Kirby to carry out her cold-blooded plot.

"In Miss Kirby's haste to cover up her deed, she was forced to leave the wires and other implements required in her wastepaper basket. Despite her feeble attempt to conceal the wires under freshly crumpled-up sheets of blank paper, Dilpate found the implements there. So this clinched the case. Miss Scott, alias Miss Kirby, came here from Blackpool to avenge her father's death."

After polishing off his biscuit, Renyalds said, "Sterling analysis, von Stray. That certainly settles the hash."

I joined in. "Yes, brilliant."

"There's more," resumed von Stray. "She obtained a position at the bank, working hard and succeeded in becoming Derrycastle's secretary. This was just the chance she was waiting for. She carefully planned the crime and executed it with precision. After Gogan left, she waited until she heard Derrycastle pick up the receiver. When she heard a dull thud, she went into his office, disconnected the wires she had arranged, and hung the receiver back onto the telephone. She left Derrycastle where he had fallen behind his large desk."

Noting Renyalds's astonishment, I saw the need to bolster von Stray's analysis of the events. "Von Stray's correct, Inspector. This has always been the only logical conclusion. Further, once we ascertained that no one but Miss Kirby could have entered or exited Derrycastle's office without access to the deadbolt, this left only Miss Kirby as the possible culprit. As I have said many times, 'Crimes that…er…resist circumstantial evidence…er…often invite false instances.'"

Renyalds raised his chin and said to me with the utmost sincerity, "That's always been my crime-fighting creed, Professor."

I let von Stray wrap up our analysis of the crime.

"This method of murder was a clever move on Miss Kirby's part," my able colleague resumed, "because it left the police baffled as to how Derrycastle was electrocuted. As you noted, Inspector, his office had not as yet been updated with electricity. Yet the puzzling fact remained that the police surgeon corroborated Dr Kenyard's on-scene cause of death by electrocution. After concealing the implements used, she ran into the outer office screaming to the clerks that Derrycastle was dead. Later, she told the police that during the time she was in Derrycastle's office sitting in the chair in front of his huge desk, she had no idea anything out of the ordinary was wrong."

Renyalds made a square fist and pounded the surface of his desk with excitement. "Amazing! I knew we could untangle the clues if we pulled the right strings! They don't call me the 'Old Foxhound' for nothing."

"If you wish, Inspector," I offered, "we will give you full credit for solving this unspeakable crime."

Von Stray was speechless over my generous suggestion.

"Thank you, old man," said Inspector Renyalds, nearly crushing my hand with both of his. "A little kudos from the super never did a hard-working public servant like myself any harm. But getting back to Miss Kirby, since we haven't incarcerated her yet, she may attempt to escape. We better head down to her flat now and arrest her with all available dispatch."

* * *

The three of us were soon on our way to No. 2½ Denton Street. Von Stray turned on the police car's radio just in time to catch the following announcement: "*Car 12, rush immediately to Denton Chambers. A lady is about to jump from the roof. That is all.*"

Von Stray turned down the radio's volume and said, "Quick, Inspector, or we may be too late!"

When we arrived, we found a huge crowd gathered around Miss Kirby's apartment building. We followed von Stray as he fought his way madly through the crowd and rushed up to the roof of the building. We were just in time to see Miss Kirby throw herself from the roof to inevitable destruction on the street below.

In Miss Kirby's parlour, von Stray found a note penned under her real name, Miss Eunice Scott. The note sat against the porcelain vase holding what was now a wilting lily. He read the note aloud.

> *To Whom it may Concern:*
>
> *I, Eunice Scott, have avenged the death of my father, A. F. Scott, by killing D. P. Derrycastle, the man who swindled my father and hastened his death. There is nothing more to live for, as my mother passed away two years ago.*
>
> *Hoping to see you all in eternity,*
>
> *Miss Eunice Scott, alias Miss Kirby.*

* * *

Later that evening, back in our comfortable lodgings, von Stray and I sat in our respective easy chairs overlooking a quiet Berkeley Square. Snifters containing a delightful French brandy accompanied us.

"Well, Dilpate," said my companion, pinching off a heap of tobacco he kept in the compartment of a miniature banyan-wood elephant, "this unhappy affair did not come out exactly as I wished. Nevertheless, Gogan is cleared of all wrongdoing, so there is some justice after all."

I sniffed my brandy and then nodded at the portrait of Captain von Stray. "Indeed. No doubt Inspector Renyalds and Scotland Yard will be calling on us again considering how quickly we cleaned up this mysterious case."

"Yes, Dilpate," von Stray said, smiling as he raised his snifter to me, "*we* certainly did."

III

A Little Birdie Tells Von Stray

Andrew McAleer

From the Desk of
Professor John W. Dilpate
Berkeley Square, London
28 August 1924

A Little Birdie Tells Von Stray

If I live into my hundredth year, I don't think I will ever forget a single detail concerning the puzzling case of "A Little Birdie Tells Von Stray." The events surrounding this intriguing affair rank as one of the most sinister and gruesome mysteries my colleague, the great private detective and criminologist Henry von Stray, ever solved on behalf of Scotland Yard.

Our involvement with the case began when our dear friend Inspector Bernard Renyalds of the Yard, summoned us to Fairfield Court located in County Durham, shortly after he'd examined the remains of a beautiful young heiress found dead in the Manor House's locked wine cellar. The Inspector became particularly baffled after he'd discovered the victim held in her right hand a strange object now identified in the official Yard record—thanks to von Stray's ingenious methods of psychological analytical crime detection—as the unfortunate soul's "dying clue."

The puzzling affair began on the 15th of March 1924, and although London's weather had been brisk that morning, I still managed to complete my morning scientific physical Indian club training exercise regimen in the Berkeley Square Gardens; a stone's throw from the lodgings I share with von Stray at 121B Berkeley Street.

While attempting to cross Berkeley on my return home, I happily yielded way to a slow trotting carter and his old horse. After the War the peaceful sight of a carter toting his wares along the streets of London had become a rarer and rarer treat in this modern age of machinery. With great effort the ancient carter straitened out his hunched back and tipped his torn and frayed slouch hat to me. I raised my Indian clubs in honor of the old gent and his faithful companion leading the sluggish charge. "Keep up the good fight, Loyal Sons of England. Never surrender!"

No sooner did I speak these words than I observed a young man in uniform pedaling a push-bicycle pell-mell down Berkeley Street from the direction of the Piccadilly. He stopped abruptly at the ground entrance of our flat, swung his right leg hurriedly over the push-bicycle's cross bar and leaned the contraption with little care against the ornamental wrought-iron fence adorning the front of our apartment building. The coast now clear of the ancient carter, I dashed across the street and approached the unexpected visitor. He was gasping for air, desperately attempting to regulate his breathing.

"May I help you, young man?" I said, bracing his shoulder.

"Tel…telegram, sir," he swallowed and then took in a generous batch of air before completing his mission. "Telegram for Mr. Henry von Stray…. From Scotland Yard, sir!"

"Great Scott!" I exclaimed, digging out two three-pence coins and handing them to the lad in exchange for the telegram.

I double-stepped it up to the first floor and hurtled my Indian clubs onto my easy chair overlooking Berkeley Square. I then located my companion in the kitchen where he was busy at the breakfast table lathering a homemade raisin scone with dollops of wild beach plumb jam shipped to him from Brant Rock, Massachusetts by one of his mysterious acquaintances.

"Good morning, Dilpate," he greeted, in his customary cheerful manner. "I trust your morning exercises have earned you a hearty breakfast?"

"Indeed," I said, eyeing my companion's tempting spread of scrambled eggs, scones, bacon rashers and kippers, "but I'm afraid you may have to sacrifice the second half of your scone." I handed him the telegram. "Urgent telegram from Scotland Yard!"

"Thank you," he said, dabbing his neatly trimmed moustache with his favorite Irish linen breakfast napkin.

I poured myself a cup of piping hot coffee. I know of no one who makes finer coffee than von Stray. The secret he claims is the proper ratio of eggshells to coffee grounds.

He opened the envelope and read its contents aloud:

"VON STRAY -(STOP)- IMMEDIATE ASSISTANCE REQUIRED -(STOP)- LORD BEACHLY'S -(STOP)- DAUGHTER? -(STOP)- RENYALDS"

He sprang out of his chair. "Pack your kit, Dilpate. We must catch the next passenger train to Durham."

"What does the telegram mean?" I enquired, blowing on my coffee. "Rather cryptic."

My companion was already clearing dishes into the sink. "It means our dear friend Inspector Renyalds is once again up against a knotty puzzle requiring our assistance in solving a possible murder."

"'Possible murder!'" I roared, pinching off a healthy ration of kippers before stuffing the rest of them into the icebox. "You never cease to amaze me, von Stray. How do you draw such a conclusion? There's nothing in the telegram regarding murder."

"Indeed there is, Dilpate," he said, now slicing a scone in half and covering the bottom half with eggs and a heap of bacon rashers. "In order to maintain secrecy and discretion in such communications, I developed a simple code with the Inspector. You will note by the telegram's instructions he requires our *immediate* assistance at Lord Robert Beachly's. His Lordship's estate, Fairfield Court, is located in Durham."

I finished chewing. "Lord Beachly—isn't he the scientific engineering chap now serving the Crown as some kind of Special Envoy to something or other? Seems everyone's being appointed as a special envoy these days. We'll start tripping over them soon."

"Quite right, Dilpate. I understand he distinguished himself more than once in the Second Afghan War. Now he and his handsome war record, along with his ingenious discoveries in the field of magnetic wave motion, have been conscripted by the Empire to be used as a Special Envoy to the Minister of Foreign Wireless Communication—an extremely important post I'm sure in this amazing age of nearly instantaneous communication."

"Yes," I agreed, thinking about my struggling carter friend as I quickly plopped the basket of scones into the breadbox, "everyone's off in such a dashed hurry these days."

My companion covered the eggs and rashers with the top of the scone and wrapped a clean napkin around the makeshift sandwich. "The matter concerns Lord Beachly's daughter. By prearrangement with the Inspector, he is to use the word 'immediate' only in matters concerning homicide. Based on his communication, I regret to say Lord Beachly's daughter, Lady Felicity Bootle, has died under mysterious circumstances. Mysterious enough for the good Inspector to require my private investigation services."

With great restraint I cleared the remaining breakfast food into the icebox without so much as sampling a single morsel—with the exception of a few bacon rashers. Naturally, Inspector Renyalds' immediate assistance took precedence over my clambering stomach. "Lady Felicity…?" I murmured thoughtfully. "Seems to me I read something about her in the *London Star* not long ago. Oh yes, tied the knot with that Sir George Stewart Bootle bloke. Fellow who's made a bundle selling cork stoppers."

"That's the one, Professor. He and Her Ladyship married in January," my companion confirmed while splashing water onto his dishes and then sliding them into their respective slots of the draining board. "No doubt her death is a sad end to a business arrangement made in Heaven."

I shook my head. "Quite tragic indeed. Er…you said, 'possible murder', von Stray. Wouldn't your telegraphic code mean she has in fact been murdered?"

"Not necessarily. There is a question mark after the word 'daughter.' By this I surmise the good Inspector is unable to determine the cause of death with complete certainty; hence, another reason for his summons."

"Good Heavens! You can't mean the dear creature may have taken her own life?"

Von Stray rubbed the deep scar located on the upper left side of his forehead—a frequent reminder of his service in the trenches during the War. "We must consider it a possibility, Dilpate; one supported by Inspector Renyalds' discreet use of the telegraphic code. Considering Lord Beachly's high-ranking position, he naturally wishes to attract the least attention possible."

He glanced around the kitchen giving it a quick inspection. "All ship-shape here, old man. Many hands make light work. Now, off to Durham," he announced vigorously while handing me the makeshift sandwich he'd assembled. He then dashed off to fetch his old, battered leather bag full of investigative tools, his overnight Gladstone bag, walking stick, and ancient wool-tweed scally cap.

* * *

I regret to report that von Stray succeeded in making our passenger-train ride to Durham most unremarkable. Rather than using the time to rest and gather his strength for the ensuing investigation, he spent the journey shilly-shallying over a pile of his scrapbooks containing tattered newspaper columns, dog-eared magazine clippings, and various articles concerning arcane subjects such as wireless communication, the cork industry, and the Minister of Foreign Wireless Communication.

"Here's an interesting item from a 1916 edition of the *London Star*, Dilpate," my companion said, interrupting my catnap. "Seems while the Imperial German Navy was piling up on you and Britain's Royal Navy Grand Fleet during the Battle of Jutland, our present fearless Minister of Foreign Wireless Communication, Lord Nigel Todhunter Slough, was accepting an important post on the Sword and Crumpet Club's Rare Cheese Committee."

"Well," I responded, stifling a yawn, "I suppose we all had to make sacrifices during the War."

* * *

We arrived in Durham by early afternoon and taxied to Fairfield Court. In the estate's forecourt we were met at once by a forlorn looking Inspector Renyalds and the estate's butler, Hinckley. Hinckley looked every bit the old guard butler in dress and stature. With seemingly little effort his stern countenance supported an unusually high forehead, and his long, thin lips were contorted in such a manner it looked as if he spent the better part of each morning biting the inside of his mouth. After brief introductions from Renyalds, Hinckley dutifully gathered our belongings and with measured steps carried them inside the Manor House.

Judging by his red face and watery eyes, Renyalds had been waiting for us in the cold for some time. His muscular shoulders were noticeably bowed, and he kept tugging nervously on his thick-red moustache—also noticeably drooping. Following a harried greeting he got down to business. "Eh…you'll have to wait on Lord Beachly. He's expecting an urgent telephone call from the Foreign Office."

"Telephone call," I protested. "Can't the Foreign Office allow the poor man to mourn the death of his daughter?"

Von Stray leaned into his walking stick given to him—readers of these chronicles will recall—by the great American Stage actor Barney McNulty. "I agree, Dilpate, the world should stop and reflect during such tragic times, but we must keep in mind that Lord Beachly's work as Special Envoy to the Minister is extremely important. This urgent telephonic communication he awaits may concern matters involving vital national security."

Renyalds stroked his moustache before speaking. "I'm afraid you may be on to something, von Stray. Anyway," he continued, wagging his right index finger toward the sky, "I got it straight from the top Lord Beachly is not to be disturbed until he's good and ready. All right by me because I want you first to have a look at Her Ladyship's remains. Condition of the corpse is rather irregular," he said, now mashing his hands together and then blowing heat into them. "Afterward we'll inspect where her remains were found. Most puzzling case I've ever encountered. Ghastly. Lady Felicity found hanging in a locked wine cellar with a death grip on a badminton shuttlecock of all things. Room locked up tighter than old man Scrooge's last shilling and of all things a full cask of wine standing on end blocked the door from the inside." He removed his derby and ran a hand through his thick crop of red hair. "I can't figure how the deuce all this played out no matter what angle I ponder. I'm over a barrel, if you'll pardon the expression. My superiors will be quite vexed if I don't provide them with some answers soon, von Stray."

My dear friend tapped Renyalds' shoulder with the ivory handle of his walking stick and then held up his black leather bag. "Let's have a look shall we and see if we can't help with your predicament. She was found holding a shuttlecock you say?"

"The Medical Examiner Dr. Colchester and I found it mashed in her left hand."

I was gobsmacked. "How the devil would a shuttlecock find its way into her hand? Sounds like the type of trick only a fiend would pull in order to send some cryptic, ghoulish message."

Renyalds shook his head. "Nothing like that, Professor. I have another theory we'll discuss later. Right now her Ladyship's corpse is resting in a cold storage room located in the cellar and I need von Stray to give her the once over before Dr. Colchester returns. He's quite anxious to get her to the morgue to carry out a postmortem." He refitted his derby. "I think it best we make access from the courtyard entrance out back. The grieving father and husband don't need us stampeding through the house any more than we have to. You can question them after I run you through the paces, von Stray."

Renyalds led us down a long driveway sweep; it ended in a cobblestone courtyard large enough for teams of wagons or motor vehicles to engage in shipping and receiving. From here one could see much of the estate's magnificent landscape. The view of endless billowing hills blanketed with sod and boarded off with hulking oak, ash, and birch was breathtaking. It was a delight to see so many mature trees not lost to industry. To our right stood a stable, and to its left a tin-roofed shed about ten feet by ten feet. Smoke belched from a stovepipe chimney fitted through one of the roof's sheets.

Outside the stable a young man with the type of square shoulders one earned from a steady life of physical labor, ran a currycomb over a handsome-looking draught horse. I couldn't hear what he was saying, but the man appeared to be talking to the horse as if he and the beast were old mates.

"Strange," I said to von Stray, casually extending my chin toward the man, "why would that chap tend to the poor animal outside in this cold when he could carry out his tasks inside the stable?"

"I find it curious also, Dilpate," von Stray spoke softly while fingering the left corner of his neatly trimmed moustache. "He must have his reasons. In any event, the man seems to enjoy his work. Judging by his friendly chum chatter with the horse they appear on excellent terms."

Renyalds shifted his stance to get a better look at the man. "That's Fairfield Court's farrier…" he started to explain before removing a notepad located in the inside pocket of his overcoat, "…Paddy O'Brian. Now let's get out of this cold, shall we? You can question him later if you think it necessary, but I've covered that barren ground."

He directed us to our immediate left by a set of large bay doors. They were swung open and pinned against the fieldstone foundation of the Manor House. A police constable paced under the doorframe periodically clapping his hands and stomping his feet to keep warm against the frigid winds. "Gentlemen," as way of introduction Renyalds held out an open palm in the direction of the constable, "Police Constable Edward Reigate—first on the scene. I have his statement, but I imagine you'll want to chat with him after I bring you up to speed."

My companion nodded at Reigate. "Good afternoon, Constable. I look forward to hearing your observations and insights in connection with this case."

Reigate touched the rim of his helmet. "An honor, sir. Thank you."

Renyalds was about to sweep past Reigate when he suddenly halted. "I thought I asked you to keep guard by the wine cellar door?"

Reigate patted his chest. "My lungs, Inspector. Needed a bit of a breather from that foul stench," he groaned, jerking his left thumb toward the interior of the cellar. "The Crown doesn't issue gas masks for wine cellar duty."

Renyalds was firm. "Watch yourself, Constable."

"My apologies, Inspector. But I swallowed enough of the Kaiser's poison in the trenches. Sort of stirs things up a bit when I smell that smell."

Renyalds paused and exhaled. "It does, son. Carry on."

* * *

Renyalds led us down a straight passageway wide enough for a horse-drawn wagon to pass through with room to spare. The electric lighting system did little to liven the crypt-like atmosphere borne from the damp, musty smell of ancient earth and cold concrete foundation walls and floor. With each step toward our destination, a noxious odor grew stronger—the distinct odor of ammonia. I now understood Reigate's need for an outside refresher and why the bay doors were left open in this cold. After approximately ten paces, Renyalds stopped, pulled the handle of a heavily insulated door to our left and we entered a cold-storage room.

With the overhead electric light already burning, Lady Felicity's remains came instantly into view. Although I've worked on numerous murder cases with von Stray, I don't think I will ever get accustomed to the shock of seeing a murder victim. There before me, laying on a long king board supported by two sawhorses, was the cold rigid body of the once beautiful and lively Lady Felicity; her knees inexplicably frozen in a slight crouching position under her canary-yellow silk night robe. Matching silk slippers complemented her robe. Hours earlier this young lady of high society had every expectation of enjoying a long life brimming with joy and happiness. Now, this comely young woman, not more than five and twenty, lay there on a jury-rigged slab; reduced to a bluish-purple object of study waiting in queue for entry into medical charts, police reports, and sensational newspaper columns.

Von Stray went straight to work and in quick order dismissed the possibility of suicide. "You say Lady Felicity was found hanging, Inspector?" He enquired, studying the right side of the victim's head. There was no question in my mind that the horrific deep-purple ligature mark extending around her chin and jowls is what drew the great detective's interest.

"Correct," confirmed Renyalds. "You were in London. It would've been a sacrilege to leave her remains in such a state. We made these temporary arrangements so you could examine her."

"I quite understand."

Renyalds felt the need to explain his own swift arrival on the scene. "As luck would have it, I was close by in Crook handling another complicated affair. Quite intricate. Cleared it up in a jiffy, so I won't be dragging you off to Crook anytime soon for your assistance on that rather difficult and complicated case." He turned to me and whispered confidentially, "Quite baffling indeed, Professor, however I settled the hash but quick."

Whatever matter the Inspector had resolved in Crook with such dispatch sounded fascinating; nevertheless, von Stray and I remained focused on our present assignment.

"Lady Felicity was in the habit of wearing lipstick," von Stray said, still hovering around her head. "Most of it has been removed, probably in preparation for sleep, yet a slight shade of pink remains on her lips. Query, Inspector: Other than moving her body here and removing the shuttlecock from her left hand, is everything exactly how you found her remains?"

Renyalds yanked his collar away from his neck. "Exactly, von Stray. In fact, we didn't even have to adjust the noose to slip her head out. The way I figure it, with the shuttlecock occupying one hand, she was unable to tighten the noose single-handed."

Von Stray announced, "I'm quite confident we can eliminate suicide."

The Inspector's eyebrows nearly vaulted through the brim of his derby. "How can you deduce that, von Stray? You've scarcely had a look at her."

Von Stray straightened up and faced Renyalds. "Gravity is the short answer to your question. Take a look at this contusion on the right side of her forehead." Renyalds moved in for an unobstructed view. Von Stray continued. "She was struck with some type of blunt instrument causing not only this contusion, but a small break of her skin resulting in her bleeding from the area in question. You will observe this dried streak of blood traveling directly from her forehead and ending in line with the top portion of her right ear. I submit that Lady felicity was on her back long enough for the stream of blood to travel downward and ultimately drying; hence revealing its course of travel. If she had remained standing after the blow, the blood would've traveled downward ending somewhere around her right jaw line."

Renyalds adjusted his tie and nodded. "Well done, von Stray. Your analysis independently confirms my theories. Never hurts to obtain a second opinion. Er…what else do you observe?"

"If indeed Lady Felicity was rendered unconscious as a result of the blow, then we must ask ourselves why she remained on her back for a period long enough for this streak of blood to dry in this manner. We know that even if the blow caused her death, it did not do so instantly since she bled. Had death been instantaneous she wouldn't have. Therefore, our tell-tale streak of blood would not exist."

I exhaled and challenged my companion. "Isn't it possible Lady Felicity's contusion was caused by an accidental bump and when she awoke committed suicide?"

"Possible, Dilpate, yet unlikely when you consider she is still wearing her slippers. You will recall how Inspector Renyalds confirmed this is exactly how her remains were discovered."

"That's true, von Stray," Renyalds agreed. "I also found it rather strange her slippers were still on her feet. Eh…I'll let you explain their relevance to Professor Dilpate. Don't want my analysis to influence your own."

"Most considerate, Inspector. The slippers have no heel backing. They are specifically designed to slide on and off easily without having to use one's hands to pull them on and off. Had she been hung while conscious—even if she intended to take her own life—the slippers would, in all probability, have fallen off."

I remained doubtful and pointed out how my companion's slipper supposition overlooked the obvious. "But even if she were deceased when hung by a supposed culprit, wouldn't the slippers still have fallen off? As you remarked earlier, 'gravity is the answer.'"

"Point well taken, Professor," von Stray said, removing his folding rule from his investigative bag, "yet the fact remains the slippers did remain on her feet. Remember, it's quite difficult to lift a corpse or unconscious person. I'm willing to wager the culprit in haste hung the rope too low to the floor and as a result her feet remained on the ground when her head was inserted through the noose. This would also explain the slight buckling of her knees."

"Quite true," Renyalds interjected. "Her slippers were still on her feet and flat on the wine cellar floor. Her knees slightly bent like a frozen puppet."

Von Stray opened his slide rule and began taking measurements of the body including one from the lurid ligature mark under her chin to the souls of her slippers. "Little doubt remains," he said, continuing to measure, "she was either unconscious or dead when hung and the pernicious deed was executed by hands other than her own. Under more scientific conditions the police surgeon should be able to make the ultimate determination on this point. In the meantime, prudence demands we proceed under the theory Lady Felicity was murdered."

Von Stray finished taking measurements. "Inspector, were photographs taken of her remains?"

Renyalds expanded his barrel chest. "Certainly! The Yard learned its lesson straightaway after the unfortunate event involving that charming Italian acrobat."

The lack of proper photographs taken during what the *London Star* bombastically referred to as "The Flying Buttress and the Battered Bobby," remains a sore subject with me.

"I should hope so, Inspector," I said, addressing him sternly. "It's a good thing von Stray and I were called in on that case, otherwise that fine young Police Constable would never have seen the return of his official police helmet."

Renyalds removed his derby, held it over his heart, and let out a long sigh. "One of the Yard's darkest hours, Professor."

I was about to pursue the matter further when von Stray requested my assistance. "Pray, Dilpate, would you be so kind as to loan me your spectacles?"

"Please be careful," I groaned, gently removing them and handing them to my companion. "You know how delicate the frames are."

To my relief he donned the spectacles carefully. He then bent over and inspected the shuttlecock resting near Lady Felicity's left hand. It was your standard cone-shaped badminton shuttlecock consisting of white goose feathers; the fat end of their shaft tips each sandwiched at graduating angles into a rounded cork head.

"Von Stray," I said, excitedly, "I was unaware shuttlecocks contain cork! Perhaps Sir Bootles—"

"Indeed, Dilpate," the great detective cut in before verifying the object's origin. "This is the shuttlecock in question I take it, Inspector?"

"Correct, von Stray. I doubt you'll find its of any importance after you hear what my investigation has uncovered thus far regarding this most unusual subject of shuttlecocks. Notwithstanding, I figured you'd want to have a gander before I mark it into evidence."

"Splendid, Inspector. I look forward to your shuttlecock report."

Moving on from the shuttlecock, Von Stray angled his head to get a look into the left pocket of Lady Felicity's night robe. Not appearing to find anything of interest, he repeated the process with her right pocket. "Hallo! There's something inside her right pocket. Appears to be a slip of paper." He removed a set of tweezers and an envelope from his investigative bag. Using the tweezers he delicately removed the object and it was indeed a folded slip of stationery paper. When he held it up for inspection, I couldn't have been more astounded.

"Von Stray," I exclaimed, "it's completely blank!"

He slid the blank paper into the envelope and handed it to Renyalds. "You'll want to mark this clue into evidence, Inspector."

"Well, von Stray," Renyalds responded with levity, "this blank piece of paper ought to clap irons on the perpetrator. Tell you what I'll do, when the time comes, I'll let you read its contents into the court record."

"I quite agree, von Stray," I said, joining in on the Inspector's fun. "No need to weigh down the scales of justice with red herrings."

The great criminologist said, while rubbing his scar, "We shall see, gentlemen. Time will tell whether or not this discovery bears any indelible mark on the case. It may mean nothing—it may mean everything."

* * *

After our examination of the body Renyalds led us out of cold storage and another ten paces down the passageway. We were now at the wine cellar approximately twenty paces beyond the bay doors. To the left of the wine cellar a set of granite stairs led up to a closed door. I later learned this door led to the kitchen. Little did I know it at the time, but in the kitchen, I would soon play a vital role in helping unravel this singularly peculiar mystery.

The wine cellar's solid oak door stood open about halfway. It swung inward to the left. Our position now placed us deep into the interior of the Manor House with its ground floor directly above us, supported by an exposed post and beam structure.

Renyalds reached into the wine cellar to his right past the doorjamb and switched on the room's electric light. "Powerful strong stench in here needs more airing, but I dare not push the door all the way in and further disturb the location of the cask blocking the door. Slide in, gents and have a look."

We did so and Renyalds followed.

The electric light fixture was attached to one of the overhead live-oak beams criss-crossing the room. The low-wattage bulb left the room quite dim.

Von Stray lifted his head a notch and sniffed. "The inescapable acrid odor of ammonia. Judging by its concentration, this room is undoubtedly its origin."

I was agog. "A wine cellar reeking of ammonia…?"

"I suspect all part of this baffling puzzle, Dilpate." He looked up at a thick hemp rope hanging from one of the beams. "I see you left the rope in tact Inspector. Its height hasn't been adjusted?"

"It hasn't. We touched as little as possible. But we had to mop up an awful puddle of ammonia. We could hardly work."

"I see. Photographs?"

Renyalds raised his blocky chin. "Every square inch…eh…we learned our lesson straightaway after that delicate matter regarding the pickled herring."

Once again, the lack of proper photographs taken during what the *London Star* publicized as "The Petty Problem of the Pickled Herring," continues to make my blood boil. If von Stray and I hadn't volunteered to assist the Yard in that pressing matter, an unfortunate fisherman from Clacton-on-Sea would still be missing the oarlocks to his dingy. For the sake of our present dilemma; however, I let the matter rest.

"Excellent," von Stray complimented. He then pointed to the floor area by a stack of wooden wine crates located beside the electric light switch. "The ammonia spill appears to begin on the floor area by the empty crates. You can see by its trail it flowed to the center of the room."

Renyalds cleared his throat. "Interesting as that may be, von Stray, I suggest we get on with the investigation. Focus on the cask."

"Patience, Inspector. The cask isn't going anywhere." My companion then removed an electric torch from his bag and switched on its powerful beam. While ducking, crouching, and stretching, he scanned every corner of the room with intense scrutiny. The room's right and left side, as well as the back wall, contained racks of bottled wine. The stack of crates in question stood three high; their bottoms facing upward. But the most astounding sight remained the large wine cask pressed against the door's interior; thus, halting its full swing.

After his inspection, von Stray switched off his torch and shared his plan of attack. "I'll want to inspect this room more thoroughly for clues, Inspector. Perhaps then I can form a supposition regarding the most unusual location of this cask. As for the present, perhaps you would do us the honor of sharing your investigative findings concerning the mysterious shuttlecock. May I suggest a better-ventilated location? As you reminded Constable Reigate, we all consumed more than our fair share of venomous gas during our extended stay on the Western Front."

* * *

In the passageway, outside the cold storage room, Renyalds rubbed his eyes and then rolled his shoulders. "It's like this, and mind you I have to tread carefully here, this being Lord Beachly and all...Special Envoy to the Minister of Foreign Wireless Communication. Not to mention the horrific end of his daughter who also happens to be his only direct heir. And if that isn't enough to get my own bloody neck into a halter, my most promising person of interest in this baffling case happens to be her husband, Mr. I'll-fight-the-War-From-the-Homefront-But-Take-a-Full-Ration-of-Medals-Thank-You—Sir George Stewart Bootle himself. While we were knee deep in mud and blood, von Stray, inhaling the Kaiser's latest batch of venom and, the good Professor here dodging stealthy U-Boats, *Sir* Bootle was up to his dinner collar in rare wines and cheeses making himself a pretty penny knocking down cork trees in Algeria or Morocco, or some other foreign lands that's got nothing to do with how we do things around here."

Von Stray removed his pipe from his overcoat pocket and bit meditatively on its stem. "I quite understand, Inspector."

"Yes," I seconded, "we understand your delicate position."

Renyalds massaged the back of his neck with a hand the size of a ham. "Mind you, what I'm about to tell you is only preliminary and, as far as I'm concerned, a bunch of rubbish you can file under double-Dutch. According to Sir Bootle, it all began yesterday before tea when Her Ladyship wallops him in a badminton match—a skill he developed no doubt while glad-handing his way through India shortly before the War. Anyway, they have their own indoor gymnasium here, as these types ordinarily do. According to Sir Bootle, he and Her Ladyship have a little game of: 'To the victor go the spoils.' The victor of the match has the honor of hiding the shuttlecock somewhere in the house. A variation of the little games Lady Felicity played as a girl. If the loser locates it within 24 hours, they have the honor of serving first in the next match."

"Preposterous," I moaned. "A man with Sir Bootle's property and standing gadding about Fairfield Court engaging in puerile games. Infernal drivel if you ask me."

Von Stray whisked his pipe stem at me and countered, "Preposterous enough to be true for humdrum society types living a dully, sluggardized existence in sequestered Manor Houses. It would also explain why the shuttlecock was found on scene. The question now presented, is why did Her Ladyship maintain her death grip on the object."

I reasoned out the only possible logical explanation. "Quite simple. She was carrying it when unexpectedly bludgeoned by the culprit. Her involuntary reflexes locked the object in her hand when she fell unconscious."

"I shall keep your keen supposition in mind, Professor, yet reserve the right to take the position that Lady Felicity may have been trying to tell us something by holding onto or retrieving the shuttlecock. Keep this in mind: we haven't yet established if the victim was in fact holding onto the shuttlecock when attacked and secondly, if she fell unconscious immediately after being struck. She may have had time to retrieve the shuttlecock from somewhere. One of her robe's pockets for instance. Please continue, Inspector."

Renyalds wandered a few feet closer to the courtyard. We followed. "Shortly before midnight last night, Lady Felicity slips out of bed, while Sir Bootle pretends he's asleep. He suspects she's off to hide the shuttlecock, so he gives her a head start and then tip-toes behind. He sees her slink into the kitchen and assumes that's her hiding place. It'll be easy as pie for someone of Sir Bootle's superior intelligence to locate the shuttlecock after a good night's rest. He does an about-face and creeps back to bed, no doubt dreaming about his inevitable triumph. Just a moment, gents." Renyalds shifted his stance and pulled out his notebook. He flipped through a few pages. "At about two o'clock this morning, Sir Bootle wakes up to find no newlywed by his side. He stays in bed for a spell assuming she'd already returned from her adventure long ago but got up to tend to some natural occurrence. When she didn't return after about ten minutes, he figures he'd been double-crossed and that she'd skulked off to locate a new hiding place. Not one to be bested, he returns to the scene of the crime, peeks into the kitchen, but sees no sign of his badminton mate. Here the real genius of Sir Bootle shines through. He observes the skeleton key to the wine cellar door isn't hanging on its assigned peg of a wooden pegboard located in the kitchen. Hence, one of his brain cells reasons out with the other one that Her Ladyship's alternate hiding spot is the wine cellar."

Von Stray stopped him. "Rather unusual isn't it, keeping a wine cellar key readily available for anyone who might feel the need to quench his thirst?"

Renyalds nodded. "My very thought. And when I inquired about it, Lord Beachly responded they'd been on short staff since the War and, with only a handful of trusty servants remaining, the need to confine the key to a single keeper no longer existed. In fact, everyone at Fairfield Court knew the wine cellar hadn't been bolted up in years—until it was found locked this morning."

Von Stray bit contemplatively on the stem of his pipe. "Interesting.

Accepting Lord Beachly's statement—which I'm assuming you credit..." he pointed his pipe stem at the Inspector and the Inspector nodded in agreement, "...that the door hadn't been locked in years and that all occupants of Fairfield knew this fact—which includes Lady Felicity—then it follows logically there would be limited reasons to touch or remove the key—least of which to unlock an unlocked door."

I contributed my own irrefutable logical analysis of the mysterious moving skeleton key. "My thoughts exactly, von Stray. The only possible conclusion is that when Lady Felicity removed it she intended to lock the wine cellar door after she'd hidden the shuttlecock. Afterward, her intent was to hide the key in order to make it nearly impossible for her husband to locate the prize within the allotted deadline. Inescapable reasoning and not very sporting, I might add."

Once again, the great criminologist praised my impeccable logical analysis. "Well reasoned, Professor. I will keep your supposition foremost in my thoughts when forming my final conclusions in this intriguing case. Please continue, Inspector."

We followed Renyalds as he proceeded to shuffle closer to the courtyard. "Bright and early this morning, the key in question was hanging on the pegboard and back on the very peg it's been hanging on for years according to the cook..." he consulted his notebook, "Miss Helen Grimsby. Charming lady. Only she swears on her saintly mother's sacred grave it'd been moved."

"Impossible," I interjected. "She couldn't possibly know it was moved if it was found hanging on its assigned peg—unless of course she moved it to begin with."

Renyalds held up his left index finger. "Exactly what I concluded, Professor, until Miss Grimsby showed me. A wise one to watch that Helen Grimsby she is. Charming lady, indeed. You see, the key's been hanging on the pegboard untouched for so many years a shadow of the key formed behind it on the pegboard. Facing the pegboard, you can see the shadow of the key's notched bit, faces leftward. When she took the key off its assigned peg this morning, she again swears on her saintly mother's sacred grave, the key bit was facing to the right exposing the pegboard's left-side key-bit shadow. So you see, whoever hung the key back on its assigned peg did so the opposite way it's been hanging for years."

"By thunder!" I exclaimed. "Why did Miss Grimsby touch the key if she suspected it'd been moved?"

"Multiple reasons, Professor, and if you allow me to return to Sir Bootle's nighttime adventures you will learn exactly why." Renyalds resumed his summary. "Believing he has uncovered his partner's final hiding place Sir Bootle returns to bed. When he wakes up this morning around seven o'clock, he finds Her Ladyship is not present and further, it does not appear as if she returned from their game of hide-and-seek. He finds this strange, yet he's not alarmed. He quickly dresses and rushes through the kitchen and down to the cellar where he finds the wine cellar door locked. It dawns on him it would be locked because Her Ladyship would have bolted it shut in order to bungle his efforts. Hardly cricket of her as you say, Professor, but all's fair in love and war. At this point, he hollers up to Miss Grimsby to fetch the wine-cellar key."

"As I suspected," I said, "Miss Grimsby removed it because Sir Bootle tricked her. Obviously, a trap to get her fingerprints on the key. You're on the right trail, Inspector, keeping him in your sights."

He nodded and winked. "The old foxhound they call me, Professor. Anyway, this is when she notices the key's been moved—more accurately, taken from its peg, and at some point replaced backwards. Not knowing that anything of a possible criminal nature was at work, she removes the key as instructed and delivers it to Sir Bootle. He unlocks the door but can't push it open—something no doubt he's quite expert at—you will recall the door swings inward. Some heavy object behind the door made it impossible for him to gain entry—the cask. He enlists Miss Grimsby's assistance and with great effort, they were able to push the door open wide enough for our hero to slip through. He switched on the electric light and sees Her Ladyship hanging by her neck."

Von Stray addressed Renyalds. "Am I correct in thinking the door can be bolted only from the outside?"

Renyalds sighed as he nodded. "Another sticky wicket. I don't see how we settle the hash in this baffling affair."

Von Stray removed his cap and ran his forearm across his forehead. "So we have a victim not only locked in a wine cellar, but for good measure a cask leveraged against the door's interior. A nippy bit of work indeed."

"Right—and the cask full to the bung. Whole hogshead in fact."

Von Stray refitted his cap. "A full hogshead must weigh 500 pounds or more and there it sat square against the door's interior. You did right in summoning us, Inspector. This increasingly intriguing case presents one impossible puzzle after another. Gentlemen, might I suggest a breath of fresh air outside before returning to the scene of this dreadful crime? I am convinced another search will reveal more clues. Clues that will help bring Lady Felicity's ruthless killer—or killers to justice."

* * *

Taking a breather with Constable Reigate by the bay doors, we swapped a few exchanges about our respective duties during the War. Paddy O'Brian and his draught horse no longer braved the cold and, the stovepipe chimney from the tin-roofed shed had ceased belching smoke.

Reigate blew hot breaths into his cupped hands. "Funny bloke our 'orse friend. Whistling away in the cold blabbering on to 'is 'orse like they was old school mates. Poor old 'orse 'ardly got a word in edgewise."

Without missing a stride von Stray asked, lighting his pipe, "Could you hear anything Mr. O'Brian said to the horse?"

Reigate shook his head. "Not a bloody word made sense to me. 'Earing's not so good, sir—still have a few artillery bursts from Passchendaele thunderin' around in there. Thought I might've 'eard 'im utter something I think about 'ferry water' when 'e 'eld a bucket up for the 'orse to drink." Reigate paused long enough to remove a silver cigarette case from his overcoat's right-side pocket and produce a cigarette with his left hand. Von Stray lit it for him. "Much obliged, sir," Reigate said, exhaling a mixture of smoke and cold while gazing at the spot Paddy O'Brian earlier occupied. "Strange man indeed, but you know, gents, it's nice to see a creature like that taken care of and loved after what they went through…. The War wasn't their scrap." He stared at the tip of his cigarette for a moment, dropped it onto a cobblestone, and mashed it out with the toe of his boot. He then looked up at the expanse of countryside surrounding Fairfield and tightened his lips. "Some would say it wasn't ours neither."

* * *

Inside the wine cellar Renyalds and I watched as von Stray made further inspection of the room; his electric torch illuminating the smallest details. As usual he borrowed my spectacles to magnify his examination of minute areas. Anticipating this tiresome habit of his, I brought along a spare set so I could keep a keen eye on his unique investigative techniques.

"This is interesting, gentlemen," he said with some curiosity while inspecting the stack of wine bottles against the left wall, "note how the wines on this rack are primarily English and French with many vintages dating back to the previous century. Observe the heavy accumulation of dust they've acquired." He pivoted to his right and used his torch to illuminate the racks of wine bottles against the back and right wall. "Now, observe the lack of dust on the bottles contained in these racks. They're stocked primarily with sherry from Spain, ports from Portugal and various reds from Algeria, Morocco and Tunisia. Very few from England and France and none dated before 1912."

Renyalds showed his palms. "Von Stray, how Lord Beachly sorts his wines doesn't get the cask in front of the door, the magic key back on its peg, and poor Lady Felicity at the end of her rope."

I threw in my oar with the Inspector. "Yes, von Stray. Dust, no dust, fascinating as it may be, the Inspector's right. Solve the riddles behind the key and cask and you'll have solved the whole puzzle. The only possible solution is that the wine cellar contains a secret passage. There is no other way in or out. That's where we must focus our attention, and as quickly as possible I might add—this ammonia is overwhelming."

"Quickness often upsets efficiency, Dilpate," my companion said, shifting a few degrees toward the stack of wooden crates waiting dutifully by the electric light switch for his undivided attention. "Ahh…now to my crates! Three empty wine crates stacked on top of one another with their bottoms facing upward. Two of the crates bear indelible manufacturing impressions from Portugal and the top one from Tunisia." He held the right side of my spectacles as he leaned in to examine the top crate's surface. "Take a look, Inspector. An almost, undetectable wax-drop on the upper right corner of the top crate. On the left side are several unmistakable stray marks caused, if I am not mistaken, by the tip of a graphite pencil. Each approximately no bigger than a quarter-inch in length, and judging by the diminishing width of the marks they appear to go from left to right."

Renyalds shrugged. "Okay, so someone likes to write his memoirs on top of wine crates. The wax drop and pencil marks could happen anywhere and at anytime during their exciting journey to Fairfield."

While the Inspector spoke, von Stray crouched down and carefully examined the wine cellar floor, the electric torch's beam leading the way. He suddenly stopped and retrieved tweezers from his bag of tricks along with a small paper envelope. He squatted down and, using his tweezers, delicately picked up a tiny object from the floor. He then stood up and, under the room's electric light, examined the object. "I can't disprove your theory, Inspector that the crate may have been used elsewhere as a desk; however, I rather doubt this broken tip of pencil I now hold with my tweezers made the same journey."

The Inspector bounded over to von Stray for a closer look. "Well…still doesn't get my cask in front of that locked door and the key back on its peg! That tiny bit of graphite could've ended up here anytime for any number of reasons."

Von Stray dropped the pencil tip into the paper envelope and handed it to Renyalds. "I concur, Inspector. You'll want to mark that. I agree we don't yet know whether it has any nexus to the case at bar. Nevertheless, it does have some probative value demonstrating that someone may have used this room for writing some type of document or message. And while it's true the wax drop and pencil scores could have occurred any time during transit, keep in mind that if true, then there's only a one in three chance the crate containing said wax and pencil scores would happen to end up as the top crate in this room. Further, the wax drop's ability to slip through British customs all the way from Tunisia without breaking or grinding off the bottom of the crate is remarkable. When you take a second look at the drop you will observe its bulbous shape and smooth glassy surface. The drop hasn't been flattened from bearing weight as it would have when the crate was filled with heavy wine bottles nor does the drop have any surface trauma such as scuffs or gouges, which it would when shuffled from port to port."

I sided with the Yard on this point, so I decided to rescue my friend by providing the only logical explanation as to why the wine cellar would be used as a writing den. "There's a simple explanation here, gentlemen. A member of the staff entered the room armed with pencil and candle to document wine inventory."

Von Stray embraced my supposition. "That seems a most probable explanation, Dilpate. Notwithstanding, keep in mind that everything in this room is potential evidence and must therefore, be preserved in the event it can be used to help solve this ghastly murder. Take for example the floor's surface by the doorway and cask. You will notice faint yet long and fresh parallel striations beginning several feet past the length of the door's swing space and continuing outside the wine cellar into the passageway. Note also the arc of scrapings left by the cask appearing on top of the striations. When Sir Bootle and Miss Grimsby pushed open the door, the cask would undoubtedly follow the swing path of the door. The round bottom of the wooden cask created an arc pattern over the striations as the door moved inward. Here, see for yourself."

We got down on our hands and knees to examine the area in question. The all-seeing eyes of von Stray were correct. The parallel scrapes on the floor were virtually invisible, but when you caught the right angle of light, you could see the pattern of lines starting about six feet into the wine cellar and extending about three feet into the hallway. Barely visible was the arc impression caused by the cask as its wooden bottom was sand-papered, so to speak, by the grainy concrete surface of floor as the door was forced open. It was unmistakable—the arc impression caused by the transference of cask wood to concrete floor sat on top of the parallel striations.

After the floor inspection I cross-examined von Stray. "What does it mean?"

Renyalds moustache seemed to droop a few fathoms. "It means what the dust, wax drop, and pencil tip do, Professor— 'that everything in this room is potential evidence and must therefore, be preserved in the event it can be used to help solve this ghastly murder.'"

Von Stray patted his shoulder. "I couldn't have said it better myself, Inspector. Now, several measurements are in order." He reached into his bag and removed his folding rule. "Professor, please be so kind as to document these measurements as I give them to you. And be careful not to break the tip of your pencil while you're at it!"

By the time the great criminologist completed his measurements I had documented the following relevant measurements: Door width: two feet six inches; Door height: five feet eight inches; Space between door bottom and floor: one-half inch; Striation width: approximately two feet; Striation length: approximately six feet three inches; Height of the bottom of the noose to the floor: four feet six inches.

Von Stray introduced two more measurements. "Distance from the ligature mark under the victim's chin to the souls of her feet: approximately four feet seven-and-one-half inches. Victim's height: approximately five feet four-and-one-half inches."

"And now, gentlemen," von Stray announced, "let's have a closer look at our infamous cask." He tapped the cask lightly with his electric torch. "Yes, quite full." After examining the cask he said, "With your permission, Inspector, I think we should roll the cask away from the door. I would like to test the door's full swing."

The Inspector nodded and together we rocked the cask toward the back of the room. As Von Stray opened the door to its extreme, its rusty hinges produced a most haunting screech reminiscent of an ancient crypt door.

The odor of ammonia was dissipating, yet I remained anxious to finish processing the crime scene. "Are you quite done, von Stray? We could all use a breather."

"Bear with me a while longer," he said, examining the hinges and then the door's locking mechanism. "Quite interesting…the hinges don't appear to have been oiled since the time of William the Conqueror and yet the door's lock—by your account, Inspector, hasn't been used since before the War—has been freshly oiled." He removed a small swatch of cotton fabric from his bag, dabbed it against an oily drip from the lock area, and then examined the swatch.

Renyalds retrieved a handkerchief and wiped his nose. "Bosh! Keep your nose to the scent, von Stray. It's a bit of oil is all. I'll wager a fiver Sir Bootle was a little too free sampling Lord Beachly's wine, so it was time to bolt things up again is all."

Von Stray remained focused on the locking mechanism. He swiped an oily portion of the lock with the tip of his right index finger, rubbed it against his thumb a few times and then sniffed his thumb tip. "Quite interesting, Inspector. A bit of oil indeed. Although…not the type one would ordinarily use on metals."

While von Stray's final effort at processing the murder scene showed great attention to detail, I knew beyond a shadow of a doubt his latest discovery would in no way help track down Lady Felicity's murderer. "What on earth could Fairfield's oiling methods possibly have to do with the case?"

"If my suspicions are correct, Professor, it means any port in a storm!"

With this final riddle my companion removed my spectacles and handed them to me. "By Jove, Dilpate! You're wearing new spectacles."

* * *

In the courtyard, Renyalds dismissed Constable Reigate from guard duty and instructed him to track down the Medical Examiner and advise him Lady Felicity's remains were ready for transport to the morgue. We watched as Reigate closed the bay doors and latched them shut. Although I couldn't have possibly known it at the time, I would soon find a clever way to use that same metal latch during a daring ruse to bring this macabre affair to a close.

When Reigate disappeared from sight Renyalds handed von Stray the evidentiary envelopes and said, "Eh…gentlemen, I imagine you'll want to speak with Lord Beachly and Sir Bootle?"

Von Stray slid the envelopes into his bag and then pulled his cap down tighter against the brisk winds. "Very much so if you could arrange an audience."

Renyalds shifted his stance while holding down his derby. "It's all been arranged. In fact, Lord Beachly requested your assistance shortly after my arrival on scene."

I threw back my shoulders. "Quite an honor."

"Yes, Professor. Ahh…it's occurred to me, gents, now that I've filled you in on all the particulars of the case, I must dash back to Crook regarding that other pressing criminal matter."

"Yes of course," I said, "we quite understand."

Von Stray responded, "How unfortunate, Inspector. I thought you had already resolved the *baffling* matter in Crook?"

Renyalds ran his fingers over his mustache. "A few minor procedural matters, I wish to tidy up. Won't take a moment, but just in case I'll pass the word along to Reigate that you're to have full cooperation in my absence. You won't even know I'm away." He gently nudged an elbow into my side. "Don't want our friend from Crook getting off on a technicality now do we, Professor."

"Certainly not," I agreed without check. "You can count on us, Inspector, Fairfield Court will remain in excellent hands during your absence."

After Renyalds departed we were about to make our way to the forecourt when we saw Paddy O'Brian exit the shed carrying what appeared to be a full bucket. When he slammed the shed door shut the tin roof rattled. Paddy stopped for a moment to look up at the flimsy roof and then made his way to the stable.

"No doubt 'ferry water' again," I joked to my companion.

Von Stray massaged his forehead scar. "Let's introduce ourselves to Mr. O'Brian shall we, Professor. This young man interests me."

"But von Stray, Lord Beachly and Sir Bootle are waiting!"

My companion gripped the ivory handle of his walking stick and countered, "My experience with such men of their social standing is that they prefer waiting for people with answers than those with questions. Perhaps a meeting with Mr. O'Brian will place us in the former category."

* * *

As we entered the stable O'Brian poured the bucket's contents into a trough. The horse lowered his head and began lapping. The stable contained four horse stalls to a side and at the far end of the structure the open doors offered a quaint vista of a small cottage. Although only one stall was occupied, the smell of fresh hay, linseed oil, and horse scent invited thoughts of simpler times.

"A brilliant specimen," von Stray said cordially. "I'm over the moon to see we didn't lose him to the War."

The young man smiled, immediately recognizing us no doubt as men who appreciate God's noble beasts of burden. Our new friend was a clean-shaven young man appearing to be in his early-20s with a ramrod physique complemented by large, callused hands and the kind of muscular forearms one earns from a hard, yet a rewarding life of labor. His weathered Irish scally cap sat tilted to the left of his high forehead. We made introductions and O'Brian provided us with a brief history of the horse in an accent sounding as much British as it did Irish.

"Belgian draught horse. Falcon's his name. My brother Joseph named him." Falcon stopped lapping water long enough to nuzzle his upper lip against O'Brian's abdomen and then resumed drinking. "Falcon was lucky. He's the last of the stable as you can see."

Von Stray studied a convenient wooden post prior to leaning his left shoulder against it. He then asked, "How did Falcon escape his service of the Empire?"

Our host adjusted his cap and gave my companion a curious look before answering. "Pure luck is all, Mr. von Stray. In fact, I guess you could say the War saved his life if you know what I mean. In August 1914—I was about 12 then—Falcon wedged a hoof between a couple of stubborn stones and fractured his coffin bone." He paused for a moment. "It was my fault. I should've been more careful inspecting the field. Anyway, my prayers to the fairies were answered because those stones ended up disqualifying old Falcon here for military service." Paddy gave Falcon's ribcage a few hearty pats.

I leaned in and petted Falcon's thick, light-brown mane. "How did he manage to survive his coffin-bone fracture?"

"My brother Joseph. He was the real horse farrier. I sort of inherited his title if you know what I mean. I'm what you might call a jack-of-all-trades. Had to be during the War. I was too young to serve, you see. Me and Felicity had to fight it on the home front. Anyway, Lord Beachly did his duty and emptied his stable for the Crown. Including my brother Joseph. Poor creatures—not even the fairies could save them." He now faced Falcon as he spoke. "Not one returned. Had it been any other time Lord Beachly probably would've put old Falcon here out to permanent pasture if you know what I mean, but knowing his whole stable was off to serve the Crown, he let Joseph nurse him back to health. I didn't know how he'd do it, but when my brother Joseph put his mind to something, he put his mind to something if you know what I mean. Got Falcon's hoof stabilized into mudpacks straightaway, on high calcium diet and he even made that contraption we keep in the shed to make distilled water. As you can see only kind of water His Nibs here will drink."

I looked down at Falcon's water trough. "Yes, looks quite distilled to me. Ingenious of your brother."

Von Stray lifted his shoulder from the post and laid his bag and walking stick onto the floor. He walked over to Falcon and gently stroked his mane. The horse took to my companion immediately and snorted merrily as von Stray patted. "A fine horse, Paddy. You and your brother Joseph are to be commended for saving and caring for him. I hesitate to ask, Paddy, but Joseph did not return from the War?"

He gave my companion another strange look. "You know, Mr. von Stray, if you didn't have a mustache you might pass for Joseph." The young man paused before resting the top of his head against Falcon's ribcage. He resumed. "No. He didn't return. He traveled back to Crosshaven a few months after

Archduke Ferdinand was assassinated and the War broke out. Wanted to see Ireland one last time." He looked up and pointed to a post near the far end of the stable. "That's his work coat hanging from that post there. His last day here he hung it on the same rose-cut nail where it hangs now. Hung it like it was nothing—an end of any other day. Been hanging there since. I half pray to come in some morning…see the jacket gone and him tending to Falcon like nothing happened. We came here as boys after my parents died and lived in that wee servants' cottage ever since." He pointed to the cottage located behind the stable. "Now Falcon here is all that's left of Joseph. He joined up with the Royal Dublin Fusiliers and ended up a prisoner of war in Germany's Limburg Camp. He was allowed to write two letters a month and he never failed to write me. I'm ashamed to say I was secretly glad he'd been captured because I knew the fairies would have an easier time watching over him there than in the trenches. He wrote how he was present when that diplomat Roger Casement visited the camp in attempts to enlist Irish troops against the British and into the German ranks. Casement's traitorous mission was a colossal failure. He underestimated his fellow Irishmen. They had no love for Britain, but there would be a devil to pay before they would ever turn their backs on the men they fought beside." He paused long enough to put his right hand under Falcon's chin and stroke the snout with his left. "Joseph's letters stopped a few months before the War ended. I eventually received word he died of typhus. And so ended the life of Joseph Michael O'Brian—his remains never to return home for proper Christian burial and therefore, through no fault of his own, sentenced to perpetual unrest."

When Paddy finished, we remained silent for a few moments while patting Falcon as if performing a ceremony in honor of Joseph's ultimate sacrifice for freedom and fellow soldier. Von Stray and I knew many Josephs—too many. After a few moments von Stray picked up his bag and walking stick. "We will leave you and Falcon to your duties, Paddy and thank you for your time." As we began exiting the stable Paddy followed. Von Stray had one more thought to share with him. "You were lucky, Paddy, that the German prison camp officials didn't censor Joseph's passages about Casement's traitorous mission."

Paddy's face lit up with pride. "Like I said, when Joseph put his mind to something, he put his mind to something. We had our own secret code ever since we were wee lads in Crosshaven. A touch of Latin and Gaelic slipped right under their German snouts!"

As we reached the courtyard outside the stable a whirling gust of wind rattled a sheet of tin loosely fastened to the shed's roof. I said to Paddy half joke and full earnest, "As Fairfield's resident jack-of-all-trades you'd better tack down that sheet of tin before it blows away."

He touched the rim of his cap and grinned. "I'm on the case, Professor—if you know what I mean…"

When safely out of Paddy's earshot I let my dear friend know my astonishment. "I'm surprised, von Stray. You never once questioned him about Lady Felicity."

The great criminologist said, glancing at the left shoulder of his overcoat, "What's more surprising, Professor, is how he never once questioned us about her!"

* * *

Inside the foyer of Fairfield's Manor House Hinckley collected our overcoats.

Von Stray asked him: "Hinckley, you look like a man of the world, what would you say made this offensive stain on the left shoulder of my overcoat?"

Hinckley squashed his lips into the size and texture of a prune as he scribbled his right index finger on the stain. He then took a whiff of the stain. "I'm quite certain this is linseed oil, sir. I shall see that it is attended to."

"Von Stray," I laughed, enjoying a good chuckle over my companion's sartorial mishap, "you must've gotten that stain leaning against the stable post. I detected the odor of linseed oil straightaway. So much for your attention to detail. Serves you right for resting on your oars while on the job!"

He joined in on the levity. "Indeed, Dilpate, evidence gathering can be quite the dirty business when one puts his shoulder to the helm." He then addressed Hinckley. "At first opportunity, Hinckley, I would be much indebted to you if you could perform an important task for me."

"Indeed, sir."

"Please convey these exact words to Mr. O'Brian and nothing more: 'Von Stray said to inform you that your use of the linseed oil is quite visible now.'"

"Very good, sir."

* * *

A minute and one half later we were standing in Sir Bootle's ground floor study.

Hinckley bowed slightly and announced, "I will advise His Lordship and Sir Bootle you have requested an audience." With that he glided out of the study.

As von Stray stalked Sir Bootle's study inspecting his collection of foreign trinkets, and bric-a-brac I laid him out in lavender. "Von Stray, I've never known you to have someone do your dirty work for you! You should be ashamed dispatching Hinckley to throw dust in the eye of Paddy. Besides, it was your own fault for leaning against the post."

He pulled on his mustache. "You will have to trust me, Dilpate. I would like nothing more than to learn the seeds I'm scattering in this area of the investigation fall onto barren ground."

It took me but a moment to decode his latest riddle. "I see…. Yes, quite clearly now. Ingenious, von Stray! You're springing some kind of intricate trap on Hinckley. I don't trust that chap either—too agreeable by a long shot. Don't you think you should have interrogated him when you had the chance?"

"We may do a little chin-wagging with him later, Dilpate, but I didn't want us to miss out on the opportunity we now have to inspect Sir Bootle's study without an extra set of probing eyes upon us. One can learn a great deal about a man's business habits and lifestyle from how he keeps his study."

"I couldn't agree more," I said, scanning the room carefully. "That's why I keep few things of importance in my own study."

I stood next to the great criminologist as he pointed the tip of his walking stick at a wall festooned with framed documents. "Take for example these letters of appreciation from foreign dignitaries and foreign manufacturers. They come primarily from timber concerns located in Spain, Portugal, Morocco, and Tunisia."

I was agog. "Von Stray! The collection of wines, were imported from the same countries."

"Splendid observation, Dilpate. All countries, rich in the types of trees used for the manufacturing of cork. Look how these documents thank and praise Sir Bootle for his support of the cork industry."

"Praise for knocking down beautiful trees more like it!" I interjected. "All so some bloke on a heavy allowance can swallow a taste of wine."

"Indeed, Dilpate," he said before getting back to the documents. "Observe how many of them date as far back as 1914, yet the latest ones display dates no later than 1919. This abrupt end to the letters could represent a break in ties with the cork industry."

I scoffed, waving my hand over Sir Bootle's pretentious wall of praise. "Cork industry! I would hardly call bottle stoppers and barrel bungs an industry worthy of such attention."

Von Stray took out his pipe and, after lighting it, took a long meditative draw before explaining, "Quite the contrary, Dilpate. In fact, the use of cork has become vital to our national security. Up until the late 19th century it had few uses—as you intimated—it was primarily manufactured for the use of bottle stoppers and bungs. But this fascinating age of industry and machinery revolutionized its economic uses. For example, it's used in the soles of shoes, food cap liners, equipment gaskets, carburetor and tank floats, even in cigarette tips. As one of the most efficient forms of low temperature insulation the manufacturing of corkboard insulation, now utilized for cold storage, has replaced inferior items such as straw, wood shavings, and sawdust. The food and beverage packing industries are very much indebted to cork."

I remained doubtful. "But how does a set of comfortable cork-filled shoes add up to issues of national security?"

Von Stray continued. "Among many other things, Dilpate, I regret to report it helped enable those stealthy German U-boats to pile up on you during your service in the Royal Navy. In the past two decades or so the use of corkboard has made possible the mass production of gaskets used in the automobile industry, pipe covering and perhaps most importantly—its use in ship and submarine construction! Corkboard is quite effective in deadening and dampening vibrations and sound, thus offering great assistance to those U-boats silently skulking the waters taking pot shots at you and your shipmates during the War. As you know all to well—without warning!"

I was dumbfounded. "Good Heavens! Who would have thought that a simple commodity such as cork would have such an effect on every-day life and could have dictated the outcome of the War."

Von Stray whisked his pipe stem at me. "Perhaps, Dilpate, by the end of this investigation we will be able to answer just *who* indeed."

Soon after von Stray spoke the words Sir Bootle entered. Although I had never met the man, there could be little doubt he was merely a shell of his former self. While dressed every bit the gentleman, he was unshaven, his face a waxy pallor, and his eyes, gazing into vacancy, sat buoyed in deep-dark circles. He must've been in his early forties and although a bit lumpish and quite a bit older than Lady Felicity, he was of the handsome traditional Norse type and wore a military-looking grey moustache. Presumably, bringing to the marriage name, property, and title, no one could fairly accuse Lord Beachly of being remiss for allowing Sir Bootle to pursue and ultimately win Lady Felicity's hand.

After brief introductions, and our condolences he plopped deep into his desk chair. Sir Bootle indicated with an open hand we were invited to sit in the chairs located in front of his desk. We took our seats and, without being asked, he reiterated in a flat, subdued voice everything he had told Inspector Renyalds about the shuttlecock game. When von Stray explained to him his conclusions supporting a theory of murder opposed to suicide, Sir Bootle seemed almost relieved and immediately turned to his own theory regarding the case.

"Gentlemen, I knew all along my dear Felicity didn't take her own life. There was never any question in my mind. I am convinced some evil foreign influence is behind my wife's murder. All I can tell you is that Lord Beachly's position as Special Envoy has placed him in a position where he's involved in dangerous matters relating to the highest levels of national security."

Von Stray was dignified yet firm in his inquiry. "Pray, Sir Bootle, I am most interested to hear the evidence you have uncovered demonstrating foreign influence is behind Lady Felicity's murder."

He lifted his hands and shrugged. He then scooped a cork-tipped cigarette out from a wooden cigarette box located on his desk and afterward slid the box toward me. After I declined politely, he presented his foreign-influence theory. "Isn't it quite obvious, von Stray? While hiding the shuttlecock she unwittingly stumbled onto an attempt by foreign agents to siege Fairfield Court and burgle Lord Beachly's secrets. No other motive exists."

Von Stray relit his pipe. "I see. A most ingenious theory, Sir Bootle, which I can assure you won't escape the attention it deserves."

"Please see to it that it doesn't, von Stray. Now, I will eliminate myself as a suspect by answering any questions you may have about inheritance—assuming you have any questions after you hear what I have to say regarding the nasty subject." He was about to light his cigarette when he suddenly stopped, gazed at it, and then laid the cigarette gently back into its box. "These are Felicity's own unique blend. I had a Turkish tobacconist I know make them specially for her." He paused for a moment to rub his eyes. "I loved Felicity more than anything in the world. I don't see how I go on without her. It's true she stands…stood to inherit a fortune from Lord Beachly, but I do not. Even if I did, nearly half of his fortune would be lost to those bloody post-war inheritance taxes. Such was the fate of my estate, Paget Gardens, which had been in the Bootle family for more than three centuries. I was forced to sell the family estate last fall; hence our living arrangement here at Fairfield Court. As long as Felicity was alive, I had Fairfield Court to call home. I'm not so sure Lord Beachly will allow me to remain now that dear Felicity has left me. If it will help you send my darling Felicity's killer to the gallows, I'm not ashamed to admit the proceeds from the sale of Paget Gardens are not enough to underwrite the lifestyle I'm accustomed to living. As you can see, gentlemen, it's not going to be all honey and pie for me."

To my surprise von Stray shifted in his chair in such a manner it indicated our interview of Sir Bootle had concluded. "Thank you, Sir Bootle. Professor Dilpate and I will do everything in our power to serve you and Lord Beachly."

Sir Bootle's chin collapsed onto his chest. "Thank you, gentlemen. That's all we ask. May I inquire how the investigation is proceeding?"

My companion's report to Sir Bootle floored me completely. "Quite well in fact. I have all but figured out how the little shell game with the wine cask was performed and have solved the mystery behind the spilled ammonia. I pray, however, that you will allow me a little more time to examine motive before I make full disclosure of my findings. I can assure you, Sir Bootle, it is essential that I withhold my conclusions at this time if I am to succeed in delivering to Lady Felicity the justice she deserves."

Sir Bootle rose from his chair. "Certainly, von Stray. We have complete faith in you and Professor Dilpate. Please let me know if I can assist the investigation in any way. I will ring for Hinckley. I know Lord Beachly is anxious to speak with you...when he's available. Affairs of state you understand."

Von Stray collected his walking stick and bag as Sir Bootle rang. While waiting for Hinckley my companion nonchalantly strolled over to Sir Bootle's congratulatory wall of framed documents. "I must commend you, sir. Your work in the cork industry is much admired."

Sir Bootle fiddled with the cigarette box. "Yes. Yes indeed. Eh...do you know much about the cork industry, von Stray?"

The great criminologist's head tittered. "I'm afraid my knowledge doesn't go far beyond knowing what end of the cork to pull."

Sir Bootle hesitated before responding, "Well...that makes two of us."

* * *

While Hinckley's gleaming shoes led us up a flight of stairs on our way to Lord Beachly's office, von Stray enquired, "How is Lord Beachly holding up, Hinckley?"

He paused. "As well as can be expected, sir. He has his duties."

135

We reached a second flight of stairs when von Stray asked, "How long have you been in His Lordship's service?"

We arrived at the second floor. Hinckley answered without stopping as we walked down a long hallway. "Many years, sir. Since the Second Afghan War. He saved my life on numerous occasions. I was merely a private, you see."

Von Stray's eyes met the butler's eyes level as they walked side-by-side. "I do see, Hinckley…. More than you know."

When we arrived at Lord Beachly's office door Hinckley knocked and announced our presence. A deep voice penetrating the door instructed us to enter. Hinckley looked at von Stray prior to opening the door and said, "If it wasn't for His Lordship, I wouldn't be where I am today, sir."

When we entered Lord Beachly's private sanctum, he was standing behind his desk yanking his vest tails. He was tall, lean, and appeared well beyond the age of sixty. His pure white hair was thinning yet holding its own in a valiant fight against baldness. Considering his important high-ranking governmental appointment, I wasn't surprised to find his office lacked the requisite stashes of brandy, Scotch whiskey, and bulging humidor boxes one ordinarily expects to find in the office of business back-slappers such as Sir Bootle. In contrast, Lord Beachly's office served as a place of work. Its walls were covered with bookshelves containing volumes of important scientific works and complicated timetable catalogues. I deduced instantly he was of the stiff-upper-lip type, a surviving member of the ever-shrinking class of the old guard. His only daughter had been found brutally murdered this morning under the most horrific circumstances and yet here he remained in his spartan surroundings, gallantly holding his post on behalf of the British Empire.

After introductions and our condolences, his icy-blue eyes made no secret of inspecting us stem-to-stern. Apparently meeting with a sufficient modicum of approval, he poured each of us a glass of water into clear glasses and then invited us to sit in the two chairs located in front of his large mahogany desk. He then repositioned his electric desktop telephone into a more strategic position and lowered himself into the depths of his swivel desk chair.

He held up his glass of water to the light and examined its contents before taking a small sip. Ceremony completed, he placed the glass back onto his desk, stood up, and began pacing; his arms folded. Von Stray watched him, as a jungle cat watches his prey. Finally, Lord Beachly broke the silence. "Gentlemen, I am told by my close colleague Sir Hamilton Wade Huddersfield you can be trusted. I value no man's opinion on the subject of trust more than Sir Hamilton's. This is why I instructed the Yard to summon you here to investigate my dear child's death. Her *murder* more precisely." He stopped pacing long enough to unfold his arms and wave a hand in our direction. "You needn't explain. The notion that she took her own life shall not be considered. I'm afraid I have a terrible confession to make, gentlemen. Like many great men who dedicate their lives to ridding the world of tyrants, we often neglect our own nest. Our own world crumbles at our feet—as mine has now. What could I have been thinking when I allowed Felicity to entangle herself with that rotter, Bootle. Shuttlecocks at midnight! Do you know he hasn't sold a single cork since the War!" He folded his arms again and stared out a window. Based on my calculations of the home's floor plan, he would have been overlooking the courtyard. "I'm in a delicate position. I'm afraid I have little time to mourn my daughter's death. As Special Envoy to the Minister of Foreign Wireless Communication, affairs of state must occupy my full attention. Do you have any idea what's at stake?" He returned to his desk chair and took a sip of water before answering his own question.

"There are many who believe, gentlemen, that another great war is imminent. I am *not* one of them." He made a fist and used it to pound his desk. "I believe peace can and must be maintained through strength and constant vigilance. Peace! Peace! Peace!" he shouted while hammering fist to desk. "Leave no room for doubt—foreign infiltrators threatening our national security plotted my child's death. I received approval moments ago from the highest authority, to share with you top-secret information—with the caveat we have your solemn oath you will maintain full discretion."

"You have it, Lord Beachly," von Stray affirmed without check. "And for the record there is no one I trust more than Professor Dilpate."

Lord Beachly said, after a long pause, "You are, gentlemen, no doubt familiar with wireless telegraphic communication. What you may not know is that this phenomenon can be used for more than forwarding and receiving messages. We are in the process of creating a device that will enable us, by manipulating the effects of rapidly varying electric and magnetic forces, to intercept the precise origin of electric waves generated by a wireless transmitter *before* the actual transmissions are detected by the intended wireless receiving station. In other words, we can get the goods before they get us!"

Von Stray picked up his glass and examined the water before taking a generous swig. "Pray, Lord Beachly, isn't it true that soon after Marconi became known for his efforts to develop wireless telegraphy that other nations viewed such technology as a threat to their own national security?"

Lord Beachly stood up, dropped his eyelids to half-mast and looked down at von Stray. "Eh…what do you mean, von Stray?"

"Respectfully, My Lord, it is hardly a secret that such wireless instruments could also be used to detonate explosives remotely."

Lord Beachly folded his arms and hoisted his chin. "I can assure you, von Stray, that the Minister has no such intentions to perfect such unsporting technology. Quite the opposite is true. His intention is to intercept enemy information and use it for the sole purpose of preventing further world destruction."

Von Stray rose fast from his chair in such a manner that I nearly ran for cover. Ever since his service in the trenches he has been more than a little skeptical of hobnobbing public officials and their self-proclaimed expertise on how to prevent war. "Respectfully, Lord Beachly, while I am, as a rule, dubious of governmental promises, because of your own distinguished front-line war service, I will accept your assurances on behalf of the Minister, whom I recall, fought the war off a map from the home front. He doesn't have your understanding of true sacrifice and certainly doesn't possess your celebrated knowledge in the field of scientific engineering. Nevertheless, having been summoned here by Inspector Renyalds of Scotland Yard, my ultimate duty is to assist him with his investigation into Lady Felicity's death. As such, I now give you *my* assurance that I will pursue the facts necessary to solve your daughter's murder in every possible way, but in a manner consistent with justice. If this means uncovering and disassembling some nefarious foreign band, then I will do so. I will not, however, reduce my investigation to the single notion that her murder came as the result of some plot to raid national secrets. I must be allowed to keep an open mind and use my own unique analytic methods of crime detection."

Following von Stray's address, I shot out of my chair and stood shoulder to shoulder with him—ready to run interference on his behalf. Lord Beachly's eyes became arrow slits; his face on the boil and his fists pumped furiously—we were witnessing the proverbial tempest in a teapot. He then marched around his desk at jousting speed and squared off with von Stray—chest heaving. "Von Stray," he roared, grabbing my companion's hand and shaking it vigorously, "I haven't received an upbraiding like that since I was a wet-behind-the-ears lieutenant in the Second Afghan War. Had it coming. You have my complete support."

"Most kind of you, Lord Beachly. I want you to know that with the invaluable assistance of Professor Dilpate, I am able to report the investigation is progressing as well as can be anticipated. Accordingly, I have but one line of inquiry for you." He freed his hand from His Lordship's grip, retrieved his glass of water, and raised the glass to eye level. "My Lord," he asked, "what type of water is contained in this glass?"

Lord Beachly tilted his head, and his eyes swiveled in deep confusion. "Why...eh...distilled water of course. We serve nothing else at Fairfield Court."

"Is it ever referred to by another name at Fairfield?"

Lord Beachly thought for a moment. "Another name? Why...yes...if memory serves me my farrier Joseph O'Brian—God rest his soul, murdered by the Kaiser—used to call it 'fairy' water. Why do you ask?"

"A small point of clarification. A police constable thought he'd heard Joseph's younger brother Paddy refer to it as 'ferry' water. During our chat with Paddy, he made several references to fairies, and it occurred to me the constable may have misheard Paddy's muffled discussion with Falcon."

Crestfallen, Lord Beachly returned to his chair. He turned his head in the direction of the courtyard and spoke. "Poor Paddy. I suppose I've neglected him as well. He never really recovered from Joseph's death. How could he? When we learned Joseph perished at Limburg all efforts to see the return of his remains failed. He never had a proper burial. I tried to comfort Paddy by telling him his brother's spirit lived on not only in him, but in Falcon—the horse Joseph rescued. I knew Falcon would be a great comfort to Paddy—he was just a boy and took my words literally. At first, I saw no harm in nurturing his imagination, but now I think he truly believes Falcon is some spiritual resurrection of Joseph." He turned his head away from the window and rested his eyes on von Stray. "I didn't notice it until now, von Stray, but you bare some resemblance to Joseph." As the words left his mouth his telephone rang. He maintained eye contact with von Stray as the contraption continued to beckon him mercilessly. Finally, he murmured, "That will be the Minister. Hinckley will see to your needs."

* * *

After our meeting with Lord Beachly, von Stray and I had a brief moment to converse in the hallway before Hinckley's arrival. I gripped my companion's shoulder in friendship. "I've never seen you so het up, old man! Well done. If some squashy government bloke such as the Minister, who rode the war out in a swivel chair, ever tries to use my scientific knowledge concerning the classification of rare South American beetle specimens as a pretext to advance national security, I'll slam the door in his face."

My friend took my hand. "I believe you would, Professor. And if the time ever comes, that such a reprobate temps you with an appointment as Special Envoy to the Minister of Rare South American Beetle Classifications, please slam that door one time for me!"

"Count on it!" I promised my friend without delay.

* * *

In less than a minute Hinckley arrived and escorted us to our sleeping quarters located on the first floor. His hand still holding our entrance door handle he said, "I conveyed your message to O'Brian, sir."

"His response?" von Stray asked, removing his moustache grooming kit from his

valise.

"He stared at me for a moment and said nothing, sir. Other than your overcoat is there anything else you wish me to attend to?"

Von Stray opened his grooming kit and removed his straight-edge razor. "Yes, Hinckley. I would be most grateful if you could perform a discreet mission for me."

"Indeed, sir."

"I will need to borrow Lady Felicity's pink lipstick, one of her cork-tipped cigarettes, a candle, and a cold bowl of water. The water you can bring at your earliest convenience."

He bowed and responded before gliding off, "Very good, sir."

"Good Heavens!" I exclaimed. "Have you gone balmy? What could you possibly need with those peculiar items?"

Von Stray retrieved a large cotton towel from the washroom and used it to cover the top of a Queen Anne mahogany end table. "Rather than tell you, Professor, I prefer to show you."

Hinckley arrived with the bowl of water and per von Stray's instructions placed it on top of the towel he'd draped over the end table. When Hinckley departed the great criminologist opened his investigative bag and removed the evidence envelope containing the blank sheet of paper he'd discovered in Lady Felicity's night-robe pocket. He then removed the sheet of paper from the envelope.

"Von Stray," I laughed, shaking my head, "it's more blank now than when you discovered it."

"If my supposition is correct, Professor," he said, dropping the sheet of paper into the bowl of water, "it won't be blank for long."

"You've fallen off your rocker, von Stray," I shouted. "You're destroying evidence!"

He removed his tweezers from his bag and said excitedly, "I think not,

Dilpate—look!"

He waited a moment and then delicately put the tweezers to a corner of the wet paper, lifted it out of the bowl and laid it flat onto the towel. I was flabbergasted. There on the sheet of paper plain as a pikestaff were the Latin words: *Nare sine cortice*

"It's magic, von Stray! Where did the words come from?"

"Invisible ink, Dilpate."

I was agog. "But how did you know they were there?"

"A reasonable conclusion. The latent evidence was there for all to see. And in this case smell. Combinations of ammonia, linseed oil, and distilled water are used in a German formula to make invisible ink. I considered the notion as soon as I suspected linseed oil had been used on the wine cellar's door lock. No doubt our murderer used linseed oil in a pinch to loosen its rust-frozen bolt. After all, the door hadn't been locked in years and you will recall the dampness contained throughout the passageway. When I saw the stable post appeared to enjoy a fresh coat of linseed oil, I discreetly absorbed a sample with my coat."

"Ingenious, von Stray. You never fail to make bricks without straw." I scratched my head. "Strange Paddy didn't warn you about the oil before you propped up your shoulder?"

"Quite peculiar, Dilpate," von Stray agreed, massaging his scar. "Yet consistent with his pattern of silence."

"Yes, I guess so," I said, turning my attention back to the cryptic Latin phrase scribbled onto the paper. "*Nare sine cortice*.... Seems to me I recall that phrase from my training days in the Royal Navy. It means 'to swim without the use of cork.' Life preservers are cork!"

"Precisely, Dilpate. Cork has been used since ancient Roman times to buoy novice swimmers. The phrase came into existence to designate those who no longer needed cork to swim. The phrase has been broadened over time to mean idiomatically 'to need no more assistance.'"

"Cork keeps bobbing up in this case everywhere we turn. This is obviously some kind of secret-coded message. Inspector Renyalds was right—Sir Bootle must be the culprit. In fact, it wouldn't surprise me if he and Hinckley have contrived some plot to steal Lord Beachly's research and sell it to the Germans. Sir Bootle all but confessed his desperate need for money and Hinckley would have access to ammonia and linseed oil. After all, he easily identified the stain on your coat and Lord Beachly confirmed distilled water is served exclusively at Fairfield."

Von Stray produced his pipe and filled it meditatively. "I agree, Dilpate. These men remain subjects of interest, nevertheless, the mystery of the cask must first be solved before I can execute my final plans."

"That reminds me, von Stray, what was all this business about you telling Sir Bootle you have all but solved the cask mystery?"

Von Stray lit his pipe. "It's quite true, Dilpate, yet before I put the tin lid on the subject, I must gather one more piece of evidence and I intend to do so after dinner. If all goes well the only things we have to worry about is whether Hinckley completes his mission for me and, if so, whether we can rely on my alarm clock!"

* * *

The tragic and horrific murder of Lady Felicity left all with the tacit understanding the case would not be discussed during dinner. During our course of Miss Grimsby's scrumptious turtle soup, I tried to boost everyone's spirits with a lively discussion about the classification methods I invented in order to streamline the cataloguing of my rare South American beetle specimens, but the interesting subject fell on tin ears. Lord Beachly spent most of the meal summoning Hinckley back and forth to the dining room to inquire whether the Minister had telephoned while Sir Bootle grew more and more despondent with each gulp of red wine.

After our meal my companion and I returned to our quarters. Readers of these von Stray chronicles are undoubtedly aware of how often the great criminologist relies on my special scientific skills as a coleopterist, not least of which is my ability to analyze facts and reduce them to scientific certainty. As a result, I was not the slightest bit surprised when von Stray assigned me to one of the most important tasks in the case.

I was in the washroom putting order to my moustache when I heard von Stray strike a match to his pipe and say to me, "Professor, in addition to meeting with Hinckley to see if he's procured the items I requested, I have one other matter I must attend to. In my absence I wonder if I might impose upon you to perform a vital mission?"

I quickly popped out of the washroom, nearly dropping my boar bristle moustache brush. "Indeed, von Stray!"

"It would be of great service if you would interview our charming cook, Miss Grimsby, concerning her whereabouts last evening around the time Sir Bootle alleges this purported game of hide-and-seek occurred."

"Consider it done, old man. I was going to suggest we give the cook a grilling. When would you like me to interrogate her?"

"Right now might be the perfect opportunity. She is most likely still putting order to her kitchen after dinner."

"My thoughts exactly," I said, pointing my moustache brush at him. "Allow me to finish my grooming and I shall have her on the chopping block post haste."

* * *

Approximately twenty minutes later I was seated at the kitchen table with Miss Grimsby determined to get her precise whereabouts during this alleged nocturnal game of hide-and-seek. Miss Grimsby must have been seventy if she was a day, yet still looked spry enough to wallop Sir Bootle in a badminton match.

I leaned into her. "Miss Grimsby, with Inspector Renyalds looking into another important criminal matter, I have been entrusted with assisting the Yard in their investigation into the unfortunate circumstances surrounding the murder of Lady Felicity."

She looked at me with globular eyes and puckered her lips into a tight circle. Her accent betrayed a slight Scottish lilt. "Oooh…sounds fierce important indeed, Professor."

"I assure you its importance cannot be overstated. Now, I don't wish to alarm you, but in order to be thorough we must ask everyone their whereabouts last evening around the time of the horrific events."

Just then a tea-kettle whistle sounded. She sprang out of her chair and said, "Don't go anywhere, Professor. I'll put together some tea."

She fetched a teapot from the hob, tea from the pantry, and in less time than it takes to tell, I was enjoying a piping hot cup of Earl Grey.

I sipped. "Thank you, Miss Grimsby. To get back to my service on behalf of the Yard, would you mind telling me where you were between the hours of say midnight and three a.m. this morning?"

She scratched the side of her face and smiled. "You must be starving half to death, Professor. You had a mere two portions of turtle soup at dinner. Let me put together a snack for you."

"Well…I could use a small bite."

Moments later I was smothered in piles of bilberry jam tarts with cream and slices of tinned beef of a rather good quality.

"Now," I said, biting into a tart, "your whereabouts?"

She produced a linen napkin and dabbed the corner of my mouth. "You like my tarts, Professor?"

"Scrumptious. Worthy of the Royal Warrant."

"Did Inspector Renyalds tell you how clever I was about the skeleton key? I noticed it had been meddled with and informed him straightaway. It was a very big help for the investigation, wasn't it? Did he tell you how clever I was?"

"He shared your keen observation with me. Most clever and ingenious, madam. I have a talent for noticing such details myself. Perhaps you would show me the pegboard in question."

I scooped a tart before we posted up at the pegboard.

"Do you see?" she asked, pointing to the pegboard. "This is the shadow behind the key. Formed by the morning sun no doubt shining in through the window over the sink."

"Remarkable," I said, nibbling my tart.

"I wouldn't work in a kitchen without morning sun. Would you, Professor?"

"Certainly not, my dear lady! I soak in the morning sun at every available opportunity during my daily Indian club exercise regimen."

She gripped my left bicep muscle. "You're a fine muscular man even if you are a wee one."

"Eh…to be clear, you only removed the key *after* instructed to do so by Sir Bootle?"

She put her hand on her heart. "On my honor, Professor. I have never had any occasion to touch that key whatever until instructed to do so this morning by himself."

We returned to the table where I had another cup of tea and helped Miss Grimsby polish off the few remaining tarts and beef slices. After a quick lecture on the benefits of Indian club training I brought my successful interrogation to a close.

"Miss Grimsby, I must say you are one of the most delightful and cooperative witnesses I have ever had occasion to interview on behalf of Scotland Yard."

Catching me completely off guard she grabbed my head, pulled it into hers, and kissed my right cheek.

* * *

When I returned to our quarters I found von Stray in his bed fiddling with his alarm clock. "How did your interrogation of Miss Grimsby go, Professor?"

"Honestly, von Stray, I don't think I've ever met a more taciturn witness in my life. It took a little fancy dancing, but I was able to coax the information out of her."

He finished setting the alarm clock and looked up at me. Something about him appeared different. "I knew I could count on you, old man. Please report."

"There's no question about it. I would say it's a scientific certainty beyond any shadow of a doubt. Based on my calculations, the eastern sun would most definitely shine through the kitchen window and directly onto the pegboard. This would in turn cause the wood's surface to fade with the exception of the portion of wood where the key blocked the sunlight. As a result, the area of wood underneath the key remained dark, giving it the appearance of a permanent shadow."

The great criminologist did me the honor of finishing my logical analysis. "Well done, Dilpate. Hence, your most thorough cross examination tends to corroborate independently Inspector Renyalds' findings that the key had not been removed in years."

"By Jove, Von Stray!" I shouted, unable to control my utter shock. "You've shaved off your moustache!"

"All part of my strategy to catch Lady Felicity's murderer, Dilpate. I suggest you retire. I have set the alarm for 2:00 a.m. At that time, I will share with you my plan to outfox our prey."

* * *

Moments after the alarm rang von Stray started to apprise me of his plan as we dressed for our nocturnal adventures. After hearing his scheme, I had more than my share of concerns.

"It all requires split-second timing!"

He reassured me. "Here, Dilpate, is where all your fitness training pays off. If anybody can complete the dash in time, it's you."

"But how do you know the culprit will take the bait?"

"Once it's set into the trap, I'd wager no one could resist."

In quicker time than it takes to tell we were tiptoeing through the kitchen. Von Stray stopped by the pegboard where the key was kept. He whispered, "You have the wine cellar key I gave you, Dilpate?"

I patted my breast pocket. "At the ready! Good thing Inspector Renyalds gave you custody of the evidence."

Passing through the kitchen we crept down the stairs to the wine cellar. Once inside von Stray leaned his walking stick against the wall and lit the candle procured by Hinckley. After a sufficient amount of wax had melted, he tilted the candle over the top crate and drops of wax dribbled onto its surface. He then stuck the butt-end of the candle onto the warm drops and held it in place until the wax hardened enough to hold the candle upright.

"Phase one complete, Dilpate. You have the matches I gave you?"

I patted my right-side jacket pocket. "All set!"

"Make sure you light a match precisely as I'm about to reenter the bay doors and hold it high enough to cast a glow over my face."

"Von Stray, we've been over this!"

"My apologies, old fellow."

I had never seen my companion so edgy. Although I had my doubts about his plan as a whole, I had worked out my end of the scheme with my usual impeccable precision, timing, and scientific efficiency.

Von Stray produced one of Lady Feliciy's cork-tipped cigarettes—kindness of Hinckley—and lit it using the candle flame. He then smudged some of Lady Felicity's pink lipstick onto the cork tip.

"Hinckley sure came through," I whispered, handing him his walking stick. "Mustn't forget this."

"His kind always does," he replied, collecting the stick and giving it a little wag. "Thanks for the reminder, Dilpate. The plan won't get far without this."

Leaving the passageway's electric lights off we proceeded down the dark passageway toward the courtyard. When we reached the bay doors, I lifted the latch and quietly opened the doors a crack. I peeked out at the courtyard. Seeing no one, I reported. "Coast is clear, old chap. Good luck!"

At that moment I separated the doors wide enough for my co-conspirator to slip out and double-time it to the stable. I kept the doors open a crack in order to watch his movements. He slid open the stable door wide enough for him to slide in sideways, yet didn't enter. He then sprang over to the shed, dropped the burning cigarette onto the ground outside the shed door and quietly entered.

Per our carefully orchestrated plan, he used his walking stick to reach up and repeatedly pound the interior of the tin roof as if beating a bass drum. A loud shimmering rattle reverberated throughout the courtyard. A split-second later he sprang from the shed, sprinted for the stable, slid in through his prearranged door slot, and rolled the door shut. From this moment on all I could do was pray the brilliant plan we devised worked.

It seemed like an eternity, as I kept vigilant watch on the courtyard from my assigned post. Finally, the stable door rolled open, and Paddy stepped into the courtyard; his head on a swivel. He then walked cautiously over to the shed alternating his head left to right and then snapping it back over his shoulder. When he arrived at the shed, he looked down at the burning cigarette stub, picked it up, and examined its cork tip. He threw the cigarette away and barged into the shed. As he did, von Stray came trotting out of the stable toward me. He now wore Joseph's jacket and, using a length of hemp rope as a rein, had Falcon in tow.

At this moment I hurriedly reached into my breast pocket to pull out a match, but came up with the wine cellar key, which managed to vault out of my hands. I promptly recovered, scooping a match from my side pocket and struck it against the metal latch of the bay door several times before it ignited. At the same moment von Stray and Falcon reached the bay doors, Paddy burst out of the shed and stood frozen as he looked in our direction. Thanks to my precise timing in lighting the match, I was able to hold its flame high enough to cast a momentary glow over von Stray's face while swinging open the bay doors wide enough to allow full entry for man and beast. I extinguished the match, swiftly recovered the key, and latched the bay doors shut before we ran for the wine cellar.

Arriving at our destination, von Stray led Falcon into the wine cellar and slammed the door shut. I could hear the bay door rattling open as I locked the wine cellar door with dispatch. Fleet of foot I raced up the stairs to the kitchen and returned the key to its peg. Paying close attention to every detail of our plan, I gingerly placed my index finger against the key's shaft to arrest its swaying. I then ducked behind the kitchen pantry.

Seconds later I heard banging on the wine cellar door and muffled yells from Paddy to open the door. The banging suddenly stopped. Moments later I heard someone enter the kitchen and begin riffling the pegboard. A clandestine crane of my neck brought Paddy into my view. I watched as he retrieved the key and ran back down leaving the cellar door open. I evacuated my place of cover and listened from the top of the cellar stairs. When I heard the wine cellar door creak open, I raced down the stairs by leaps and bounds ready to thwart Paddy's inevitable attempt to escape when he found von Stray in the wine cellar. When I arrived at my appointed *rendezvous* nothing could have prepared me for what I saw. There was von Stray on his knees, the candlelight flicking over him as he held the lifeless Paddy O'Brian in his arms.

* * *

"He fainted from shock, Dilpate. I'll carry him to the stable where he can be with Falcon when he recovers."

I looked at the young man resting peacefully in my companion's arms; arms covered by Joseph's jacket. I couldn't imagine how such a gentle-looking soul could be responsible for the dreadful events requiring our investigative services. "He'll need water," I sighed, taking charge of Falcon's rope.

Inside the stable we stood over Paddy as he sat on a bale of hay sipping water. Von Stray had already returned Joseph's jacket to the rose-cut nail and I, Falcon to his stall.

Paddy rubbed his face and gazed vacantly at von Stray. "When I saw you in the candlelight, I thought you were Joseph. I thought he was in there with Felicity." He swallowed a few times. "How did you know?"

"A few things gave you away, Paddy. Your lack of curiosity regarding Lady Felicity's death; the German formula for invisible ink; your knowledge of Latin. The subterfuge you employed, while ingenious, did little to help your case. During the course of our investigation Inspector Renyalds mentioned something quite interesting. He said the shuttlecock game was a continuation of the sort of games Lady Felicity played in childhood. It occurred to me when we spoke earlier that you and Felicity were childhood companions. As you did a moment ago, you referred to her as 'Felicity' excluding her title. You still see her as your childhood friend, and she saw you much the same way. Your trickery struck me as a game as much as an attempt to conceal the killer's identity."

Paddy finished his water and with great effort wobbled to his feet. He leaned against Falcon's stall and petted his friend's snout. "I thought it might give me more time. Time to buy Falcon and return to Ireland. I can't understand how you worked it out so fast."

"Your shoddy refitting of the tin sheet on the shed. The scrape marks on the wine cellar floor, are about the same width and length of the sheet. After you killed Lady Felicity, probably by hitting her on the head with a bottle containing ammonia, you then hung her body in a feeble attempt to make it look like suicide. But then, you outsmarted yourself by turning it into a game. You removed a sheet of tin from the roof knowing it was thin enough to slide under the wine cellar door. It was long enough to extend five or six feet beyond the threshold on either side of the door. You're a strong man, Paddy. You were able to rock the cask onto the portion of tin extending into the wine cellar leaving enough room not to interfere with the door's swing. You then shut the door, which could easily clear the sheet of tin flat to floor. A few feet of tin extended into the passageway. At some point you went up to the kitchen to retrieve the key in order to lock the door. The bolt was rusted—but fortunately you had a supply of linseed oil at the ready because you were using it to mix a batch of invisible ink. You oiled the lock, worked it shut, and then returned the key."

The great criminologist's explanation of the subterfuge only added to my bewilderment. "But, von Stray," I interjected, "if he locked the door, how did he get the cask against the inside of the door?"

Von Stray reached into Falcon's stall and recovered his walking stick. "You had an accomplice didn't you, Paddy? An unwitting one, albeit. You clamped harness ropes to the portion of tin extending beyond the wine cellar threshold and then used Falcon to drag the sheet. As Falcon pulled the sheet the wine cask resting on the interior portion of tin traveled along with it toward the door's interior. Once the cask pinned up against the door and Falcon continued to pull, the sheet crossed completely beyond the threshold into the passageway. You replaced the sheet of tin back onto the roof, but in your haste, you neglected to tack it down properly."

My companion's attention to the smallest details and his ability to analyze logically their potential relevance never ceases to leave me awestruck. "Amazing, von Stray. How did you know he used the tin from the roof?"

He raised his walking stick at me. "Your keen observation, Dilpate certainly played an important role in my analysis. When a gust of wind rattled a single sheet of tin, you advised Paddy to repair it promptly. Along with the floor striations, the loosely fitted sheet aroused my curiosity enough to warrant an inspection of the roof. While you interviewed Miss Grimsby, I put my electric torch to the sheet in question and saw it contained fresh scrape marks consistent with the floor striations."

I remained modest about my invaluable contribution to solving the case. "Indeed, von Stray. I also found the shoddy workmanship of the roof rather suspicious."

I daresay his indebtedness to me for solving some of the more difficult parts of the puzzle didn't end there.

"And, Professor, your observation of Paddy grooming Falcon in the cold winds rather than inside the stable also proved perceptive. Falcon also breathed in his share of ammonia. No doubt his lungs were rewarded with plenty of fresh air after his hard pull."

I humbly waved off his flattery. "I did no more than my duty in reporting the suspicious activity."

My companion walked over to Paddy and joined him in stroking Falcon's snout. "I think a great burden would be lifted, Paddy, if you told us how all this unfolded."

Paddy sat slouched on the bale of hay and stared at the floor as he spoke. "Like so many of her ilk, betrayal is in her blood. Felicity betrayed me, her country, Joseph, and Falcon. I thought she was true and honest like her father, but in the end, it was only her self-interest that mattered to her. You were right, Mr. von Stray, we were best childhood friends—I thought forever. We had formed an alliance during the War. Both determined to do our part on the home front. I was too young to fight. I see now it was all a game to her...*I* was a game. A distraction to pass idle time. She heard rumors Bootle was selling cork to the Germans on the sly. Felicity would find one reason or another to visit Paget Gardens in order to get the goods on him. At least I thought she was pretending. I think at first, she was dedicated to the cause. But as she grew, money and privilege changed all that. Sure she was going to inherit Fairfield Court and Bootle inherited Paget Gardens, but it went to taxes and relentless creditors. He made a fortune off cork only to squander it on good living. A clever marriage was the only thing that could save his name and lifestyle. Felicity convinced me the engagement was all show. She told me we had Bootle right where we wanted him and all she needed was my brother's letters where I documented all the goods on Bootle in invisible ink. She said she would put them in the hands of the proper authorities. A fitting tribute to Joseph I figured. A lasting credit to his service—his own letters bringing a traitor to justice. He wrote them in pencil, you see, and using invisible ink, I wrote down our findings about Bootle between the lines like a real spy does in order to hide their secrets in plain view. Just like Joseph did in his letters when he hid our secrets in Latin and Gaelic. I trusted her with my brother's final words and the day before her wedding I asked what became of the letters and the goods we got on Bootle." He paused and rested his eyes on Falcon before continuing. "She looked at me and said, as if discussing last week's newspapers, 'Oh those…I burned them. That War's long over and so is the game.' She saw the rage in my eyes and said, 'I could—like that—have you and Falcon sent off to pasture, if you know what I mean.' Falcon was the last connection to my brother. He's all I have."

Von Stray lit his pipe and after a long meditative draw, asked compassionately, "Would you care to tell us, Paddy, what happened in the wine cellar?"

"After I learned she destroyed all Joseph's letters I rewrote them from memory. When she threatened Falcon, I knew she could search my quarters at anytime. I used the wine cellar as my secret headquarters and hid all my work there. And when Bootle brought his wine cellar here from Paget Gardens, he outsmarted himself because the bottle labels provided me with a list of the many nations he plundered. When I finished reconstructing the letters I planned to put all the evidence against Bootle back into them with invisible ink. I was making the formula when she stumbled in on me. She said she was going to murder Falcon and have me sent away. I bashed her with the bottle of ammonia. The bottle didn't break but some ammonia spilled. She fell to the floor and reached for her little toy. She smiled at me a most devilish…evil grin. She died. She died…long ago. You know the rest."

"Why the note left in her pocket?" von Stray continued.

Paddy shrugged. "All part of the game. Who would've ever suspected an Irish servant like me to know Latin? You were quite clever in your questioning. I knew when I told you about Joseph's Latin and Gaelic code it might be my undoing." He pulled out a fistful of hay from the bale, stood up, and fed it to Falcon. *"Nare sine cortice*— 'to swim without the use of cork.' A fitting send off was it not? She no longer needed the charity of this boy from County Cork…I reject her charity for all eternity."

* * *

It was daybreak by the time we finished with Paddy. I woke Hinckley and asked him to telephone the local constabulary to see if they could track down Inspector Renyalds in Crook and Police Constable Reigate. Reigate arrived around breakfast time to take Paddy into custody.

Paddy's final words to us came in the form of a request. "You'll watch over Falcon for me?"

"Other than England," von Stray said, placing a comforting hand on the young man's back, "he's all Lord Beachly has left."

Inspector Renyalds arrived shortly afterward, and we apprised him of the events. I couldn't have been more honored when he thanked us profusely for our involvement in the case and further advised—to my great relief—that he would be taking matters into his hands henceforth.

As we were about to make our departure for London he stopped us abruptly. "Ahh…one minor thing, von Stray before you and Professor Dilpate make for the train station…"

"Anything, Inspector."

He pulled on his moustache. "I wonder if I could run by you a few minor details regarding the Crook matter."

* * *

During our taxi ride to the train station, I looked out the window enjoying a lovely view of the English countryside. I said to my friend, "I sincerely hope Lord Beachly upholds his promise to have Sir Bootle's cork business investigated by the authorities."

"I believe Lord Beachly to be a man of his word, Dilpate."

I reflected for a moment. "You know, it's occurred to me that in some ironical way, Sir Bootle's theory about an evil foreign influence being responsible for Lady Felicity's death wasn't entirely incorrect."

A veil of pipe smoke drifted by my companion's face. "In what way, Dilpate?"

"Well…if he hadn't sold cork to our enemies during the War, Lady Felicity would've had no motive to play Mata Hari and conscript Paddy into her espionage games."

He nodded. "There's some truth to what you say, Dilpate. The Chinese have an interesting saying I think applies: 'A man's sins last for three generations.' I fear the world will always produce men like Sir Bootle who believe oceans and titles insulate them from their misdeeds. Sooner or later we all pay the piper."

"Well put, von Stray. And think of all the poor trees he cut down to feather his own nest. Not to mention all these motor-cars racing around with cork engines—they're putting the poor carter out of business. It's getting so you can hardly cross the streets of London without getting pummeled by the clanking contraptions. Give me a horse backfire any day!"

"I agree, Professor. Man would be much better off if we limited the use of cork to more important items such as the head of a shuttlecock—also known as a badminton 'bird!'"

I laughed. "Yes, funny name for it, von Stray. Strange how such a funny little item and silly game of hide-and-seek led Lady Felicity to her doom. By Jehoshaphat—*bird*! It was a dying clue from Lady Felicity after all."

Von Stray whisked the end of his pipe at me. "Touché, Professor. Once I learned Paddy's horse was named Falcon, I certainly considered it clear and convincing evidence that the possibility did exist it was in fact Lady Felicity's dying clue."

"Well played, old man," I said, removing my cap and slapping it across his knee, "I guess you could say…a little birdie told you."

IV

Von Stray and the Five-Fingered Fraudster

Andrew McAleer

From the Desk of
Professor John W. Dilpate
Berkeley Square, London
29 August 1924

Von Stray and the Five-Fingered Fraudster

The present narrative would never have been written if Inspector Renyalds of Scotland Yard hadn't summoned von Stray and me to Lord Beachly's Fairfield Court estate, located in County Durham. The Inspector requested our assistance, when it became apparent he would be unable to solve a sinister and baffling case concerning the gruesome murder of a young heiress found murdered in a locked wine cellar. Readers of these narratives will recall that mystery as: "A Little Birdie Tells von Stray."

After von Stray and I solved the horrific crime and apprehended the culprit by means of an ingenious ruse I helped von Stray mastermind, we had a perchance meeting with another government official on our return home from the north. This serendipitous encounter resulted in us working on a separate and distinct matter on behalf of His Majesty's Customs Service.

It was mid-March 1924, and the good people of Durham were still battling the cold, raw effects of a particularly brutal winter. With our business now complete at Fairfield Court, von Stray and I were at the train station looking forward to returning to the warm comforts of our Berkeley Street flat in London. I was on a rare sabbatical from the University Clifford and anxious to return to my much-neglected work classifying the University's collection of extremely rare South American beetle specimens. Presently, however, we were discussing plans to unwind with a quiet tea and lunch in the train's dining carriage. As we were about to board the 3:47 p.m. train to King's Cross, an old acquaintance of ours came up to my elbow. It was none other than Captain E. M. Dumfries, a special agent of His Majesty's Customs Service and a fellow member of the Fraternal Order of Benevolent Walnuts.

Dumfries greeted me with his customary firm handshake; however, his reception seemed hurried and lacked his normally cheerful disposition. "Er… good morning, Professor Dilpate," he said, pulling a black leather glove out of his left coat pocket and quickly stuffing it into his right pocket. "Don't let me forget I put the glove in my right pocket, gentlemen. Right pocket. Professor, how are your rare beetle studies coming along at University? Wonderful to hear."

Before I could answer, he touched the brim of his battered Scottish tam and then held out a hand to von Stray. "Ah, here is my dear friend Mr. Henry von Stray himself! Eh…what's wrong with your face? Looks like you're missing something or other like a moustache or something of the sort."

"You are correct as usual, Captain," von Stray responded in his usual cordial manner. "Your attention to detail is as keen as ever. Matters involving national security in the case Professor Dilpate and I solved hours ago, led to my moustache making the ultimate sacrifice."

"Well…sorry to hear of your loss; still it is indeed an honor to see you again, my dear friend. How are you holding up after that nasty Fairfield business at Lord Beachly's, anyway? Word gets around fast, you know."

The quick-witted von Stray was about to respond when Dumfries hurriedly piloted us off the platform and aboard the train. "We must hurry now, gentlemen. Climb aboard," he instructed, while reflexively patting his right coat pocket as if conducting a quick pat search in order to make sure that the glove he had placed there moments ago had not somehow managed to spring itself from confinement.

Von Stray and I glanced at each other as if to acknowledge how we noted a sense of urgency in Dumfries' tone, yet we called no attention to our concerns until we settled in the dining carriage. We sat next to a window ready to provide us with a beautiful, panoramic view of the English countryside.

Von Stray found a convenient place for his walking stick and then adjusted his seat. "I don't want to intrude, Captain, but I suspect your mind is occupied with a troubling matter?"

"Yes," I seconded, "is anything the matter, Captain?"

He scratched the back of his head. "Er…I'm in fine fettle, gentlemen. No worries. A peculiar matter at customs has me flummoxed, is all. Nothing a strong cup of tea wouldn't remedy. Besides, as I said, I heard about those unfortunate events at Lord Beachly's, gentlemen. Well done. You needn't worry yourself over my small affair." He then murmured, "Quite a puzzle though."

Von Stray filled his pipe with a few pinches of Prince Albert tobacco and said with his usual sincerity, "No trouble at all, Captain. Always have time for others and others will have time for you. When it comes to a friend in need there is no such thing as a small affair. Moreover, as a fellow Benevolent Walnut, your dilemma deserves our fullest attention."

The brilliant mind of von Stray never ceases to amaze me. He had just solved the unsolvable case of a beautiful young woman's tragic murder and rather than dwell on its horrific details or gloat about his ingenious methods of crime detection, which unraveled the puzzle and brought a killer to justice, he was able to put the matter behind him completely. Here he was now ready to move on to the next formidable task at hand, embracing his usual interest in logical analysis.

My colleagues at the University Clifford—embracing this newer science of psychological fiddle faddle, and its latest preposterous theories before they're even off the presses—theorize that von Stray's sense of duty must be some sort of defense mechanism developed during his time in the trenches during the War. I believe their theories are existential poppycock and know his duty is borne from his never-ending quest for justice. His devotion to friendship is a derivative of that duty.

Following von Stray's lead, I joined in front-and-center. "I quite agree, Captain. No point in wasting our strategic positioning in this dining carriage. Everything smells delicious. Perhaps a bite to eat with our tea will help settle your nerves."

The Captain pursed his lips, and patted his large stomach. "Wonderful idea, Professor. Perhaps a small snack might help ease the tension."

* * *

We flanked our farmhouse tea with a bit of English nourishment consisting of beef Wellington, delicious salmon cakes, Yorkshire puddings, and a small pile of Eccles cakes. The warm tea and magnificent views of the English countryside bolstered Dumfries' spirits immensely.

Von Stray leaned back in his chair, worked his pipe up to full-steam, and got down to the case at hand. "Tell me the facts behind this *baffling* matter Captain and perhaps I'll be able to answer that question you asked me before boarding the train."

Dumfries looked at him quizzically. "Question...?"

My friend from Berkley Street stirred some honey into his tea. When traveling, von Stray always carries with him a small vial of honey. He procures it from a retired chap who went on to become a quite capable apiarist.

"You asked me how I was holding up after the Fairfield matter. Outline the facts in connection with your custom's predicament and we shall see."

"Yes, Captain," I said, still working on a cake. "Let's see if we can't clean up this case as well."

Dumfries lit a cigar and paused for a moment to arrange his thoughts. "Thank you, gentlemen. To start, an importer failed to claim and refused to pay the duty on one thousand expensive Italian leather gloves. As a result, we had to confiscate them at customs for sale at public auction. When we opened the shipment, we were flabbergasted to discover that it contained left-handed gloves only!"

"Very peculiar indeed," I said, rubbing my chin before selecting another cake. "A careless error of some sort must have been made by the merchant's clerk who shipped them. A simple message via wireless telegraph to their home office ought to clear the matter up, Captain. Don't you agree, von Stray?"

A twinkle appeared in my companion's left eye; the familiar twinkle he gets when forming a hypothesis. "Possibly, Dilpate. Possibly." He then said, "Please proceed, Captain."

"We thought the matter suspicious," Dumfries adjusted his girth, "so we searched each glove to see if any contained contraband."

Von Stray lowered his teacup and said, "I venture to guess that your search produced negative results, Captain."

"I'm afraid you're correct," he said, reaching for his teacup while heaving a sigh of defeat. "But, how did you know?"

"A simple logical analysis," said von Stray. He canted his pipe and then explained his analysis for the Captain's benefit.

"Even if the container of gloves had been claimed, its contents would most likely be examined by customs. In that event, your well-trained agents surely would have observed that the gloves were all left-handed. The result, as in the present case, would be a thorough search for contraband. Anyone attempting to smuggle contraband into the country would only run the risk of drawing further attention to their ultimate scheme had the gloves arrived without their matching partners. I'm afraid our answer to this perplexing matter must then lie elsewhere."

I finished my cake and nodded. "I agree, Captain. That leaves the only answer possible—a simple shipping error. We could dash off a quick telegram to their home office in Italy and clear the matter up in no time."

Dumfries agreed with my logical solution to the problem. "Excellent idea, Professor."

Despite my irrefutable conclusion to the simple problem, von Stray persisted with his questions.

"What became of the gloves?"

Dumfries bit into a cigar and showed his palms. "Sold at auction to an elderly vagrant for five pounds. Nice old sot. Looked a bit on his uppers. Don't know what he'd want with them."

"The old man paid five pounds for a shipment that contained nothing but left-handed gloves?" I said, not concealing my skepticism. "At any price they'd be useless."

The train came to a stop at York near Hollis Gardens.

"I'm afraid you're wrong about that, my dear friend," von Stray corrected. "Left-handed gloves of this type can be quite valuable. In fact, *very* valuable indeed...when in the right hands."

Dumfries brushed a heap of cigar ash off his chest. "You've lost me, von Stray."

"Yes, you've lost me too," I admitted.

The great criminologist drank the last of his tea, sprang out of his seat, and flipped on his ancient, wool-tweed cap. "Captain, I believe I've solved your problem. We must exit the train at once."

I reeled. "Exit the train? Von Stray you're always talking in riddles."

"No riddle here, Dilpate. If my memory serves me correctly, Hollis Gardens has the nearest customs office to Fairfield Court. This fact is plain for all to see."

"Von Stray, I don't follow."

"You will in short order, Dilpate. And you too, Captain. Come, gentlemen, we haven't a moment to spare."

* * *

We arrived at the Hollis Gardens customs house just as a customs officer was auctioning off to a vagrant, for five pounds, another unclaimed shipment.

Von Stray approached the auctioneer. "Pardon my interruption, sir, my name is Henry von Stray. This is my colleague, Professor John Dilpate. With us, I'm sure you'll recognize, is Captain E. M. Dumfries, special agent of His Majesty's Customs Service."

The customs officer adjusted his gold-rimmed pince-nez and studied the Captain, as if he were the next unclaimed item up for auction. "Yes, Captain Dumfries indeed. How can I be of service to you, Captain?"

The Captain mashed his hands together. "Well…er…"

"Captain Dumfries," von Stray cut in while pointing to the poor vagrant who had just bought the unclaimed shipment, "you may take that poor chap into custody."

"On what grounds?" the Captain asked.

"For being an accessory to this underhanded scheme."

"Scheme?"

"Yes, Captain. A clever plot to avoid paying the Crown's import taxes. If you take a closer examination of him, I'm certain you will discover that he's the same chap who purchased the left-handed gloves at the Fairfield Court auction house."

The old man stepped forward massaging his ragged newsboy cap. "Honest, gents, a man gave me *two* 'alf crowns for me trouble. Said 'e'd be out bid if anyone knew 'e wanted the shipments. I've been down on me luck you see."

"Von Stray, it's he!" the Captain's jaw dropped. "That's the same bloke who bought the first shipment. I don't understand."

"Yes. Make some sense, von Stray," I demanded. "Why are you detaining this poor old chap?"

"I'm making perfect sense, Dilpate. Open the unclaimed shipment just auctioned and you will discover one thousand expensive Italian leather gloves. Only this time, you will discover that they are all *right*-handed."

There was no need to open the shipment. The customs auctioneer confirmed my colleague's logical analysis of the mysterious shipments. Unfortunately, Dumfries had to confiscate for evidence, the old gent's two half crowns. Von Stray quickly remedied the poor creature's reversals by replacing the half crowns with two of his own and then, fortified him with a generous serving of brandy from the flask he stows in his investigative bag. Afterward, the old gent led us to the culprit who'd hired him. He turned out to be a criminal mastermind and I regret to report this wouldn't be the last time he'd cross swords with von Stray.

* * *

While waiting for the next passenger train to London, we found ourselves relaxing at a quiet Hollis Gardens pub doing justice to a scrumptious York dry-cured ham and enjoying a fine pint of Belgian ale before a warm hearth.

Captain Dumfries puffed an enormous cigar as he questioned von Stray. "How did you figure it out, von Stray?"

"Simple logic, Captain," von Stray informed him. "I formed a probable supposition when you said the importer never claimed the shipment. Then, once the notion of contraband was eliminated, my supposition was all but confirmed."

I took a sip of ale and then raised a finger. "Yes, that was the linchpin that connected the mysterious facts behind this matter, Captain."

"Correct, Dilpate," von Stray resumed, giving me my due credit for helping solve the case. "It was an ingenious conspiracy on the part of the exporter and importer of the gloves to defraud His Majesty's government of the duty fee owed on the shipment. The importer deliberately declined to pay the heavy duty knowing that he could purchase the shipments at a nominal price through a secret, unsuspecting representative."

I concurred. "Yes, Captain. This was the only logical conclusion once we ruled out the possibility of a shipment error or the gloves being used as a conduit to smuggle contraband. It was quite fortunate that we stopped you from dispatching a wireless telegraph to the exporter."

Dumfries brushed off another heap of cigar ash from his stomach. "Seemed like a good idea at the time, Professor."

I set him straight. "Such an enquiry would have given the culprits fore-warning that we had uncovered some jiggery-pokery with the shipments."

Dumfries raised his pint, tipped it slightly in my direction and said, "Ingenious, Professor, I don't know what I would have done without your psychological insight into the criminal mind."

"Thank you," I said, rather humbly. "My colleagues and I at Clifford University often discuss the fascinating contributions modern psychology is making in understanding the human condition."

Dumfries nodded. "And, von Stray, your assistance in this case is duly noted by me as well."

Von Stray raised his pint and smiled. "Thank you, Captain. Very generous of you."

"No doubt, Captain," I said, forking a slice of ham from the platter and relocating it to my plate, "your superiors at Customs will be most satisfied with your progress and ultimate resolution of the case."

Dumfries touched the brim of his tam and said, "They will indeed, Professor." He then proceeded to rub his moustache and purse his lips. "Er...you wouldn't mind, gentlemen, would you, if I leave out your small part in helping to solve the case…?"

"Not at all, Captain," I said, waving a hand of assent. "We were delighted to help the Crown bring the perpetrator to justice and exonerate the poor innocent vagrant."

Von Stray was speechless over my generosity in allowing a public servant of Dumfries' stature to receive full credit for exposing the scheme.

The Captain quickly finished his pint, as the barmaid arrived to settle up our account. As he rose from his chair he slipped on a new pair of exquisite-looking leather gloves and bid us farewell. "Good evening, gentlemen. It's been a real pleasure and honor, but I must rush off and attend to a few details."

* * *

Early the next morning at our homey lodgings located at 121B Berkley Street, von Stray sat in his easy chair near the fireplace. He appeared in deep reflection as he gazed out the window overlooking Berkeley Square. I tossed a log onto the cheery fire and sat in my easy chair opposite him. Here we have spent countless hours through the years analyzing cases while taking warmth from friendship and fireplace.

I asked, "Is everything all right, von Stray?"

My good friend bit into a piece of his homemade Scottish shortbread. Von Stray is an excellent cook. "All is well, Dilpate. Nevertheless, I can't help wondering what would have happened if we didn't have that fortuitous meeting with Captain Dumfries."

"Undoubtedly he'd still be pondering the customs matter with no solution in sight."

Von Stray's eyes remained on the Square as he spoke to me. "In fact, if the horrific murder at Lord Beachly's had never occurred, I can think of no other business that would have brought us to Fairfield Court. Hence, we might never have heard about the customs matter at all."

"Quite true," I said, helping myself to a piece of buttery shortbread. "Well then, we certainly have that ghastly affair to be thankful for."

Acknowledgements

The authors would like to thank some of Henry von Stray's best friends—Ruth McAleer, Paul McAleer, Jay McAleer, Art Taylor, Kristen Kyle, Anne Kyle, Gay Toltl Kinman, DeWayn Marzagalli, and Vincent Massey. Special thanks to Level Best Books editors and supporters-in-chief Verena Rose and Shawn Reilly Simmons. Their belief and support of Henry von Stray means everything. Very special thanks to the entire Level Best Team who work tirelessly behind the scenes in the publishing industry to make it all possible. Lastly, thank you to all the Henry von Stray fans who make chronicling the von Stray mysteries and adventures a sheer joy.

About the Authors

John McAleer around the time he created Henry von Stray circa 1930s

John McAleer is the Edgar Allan Poe Award-winning author of *Rex Stout: A Biography* and the Pulitzer nominated *Emerson: Days of Encounter.* He taught English Literature at Harvard and then Boston College for more than half a century and was also a permanent fellow at Durham University, England. McAleer created 1920s London-based private detective Henry von Stray in 1937, during the Golden Age of Detective Fiction. The Great Depression and McAleer's World War Two service interrupted the von Stray series and all the stories were believed lost until an original von Stray manuscript was discovered more than 80 years later.

Andrew McAleer is the author of the *101 Habits of Highly Successful Novelists, Mystery Writing in a Nutshell* (with Edgar winner John McAleer), and co-editor of the *Coast-to-Coast* mystery series and *Edgar & Shamus Go Golden.*

Short stories edited by him won the Derringer and MaCavity, appeared in the Best American Mystery Stories, and received multiple Agatha, Shamus, and Anthony Award nominations. He taught classic crime fiction at Boston College and served in Afghanistan as a U.S. Army Historian before returning to public service in the criminal justice system. He is a member of the Private Eye Writers of America, The Speckled Band of Boston, and The Friends of Irene Adler.

AUTHOR WEBSITE:
  www.amcaleer.com

SOCIAL MEDIA HANDLES:
  Instagram: Mcaleermysteries

Coming Soon from Level Best Books!

**Edgar Award Winner John McAleer's
Henry von Stray**

in

*A Casebook of Crime
Thrilling Adventures of Suspense from the Golden Age of Mystery*

Volume 2

Special Introduction by Derringer Award Winner Stacy Woodson

* * *

The Singular Case of the Bandaged Bobby

When a pair of heartless con artists disguised as London police constables swindle an innocent widow who fled Belgium during the Great War, celebrated detective Henry von Stray and his trusted companion Professor John Dilpate find themselves in a race against time to outwit the confidence men and rescue the poor widow from financial ruin. In the case that led to von Stray becoming recognized as one of the world's foremost criminologists of his day, "The Singular Case of the Bandaged Bobby" exhibits the great detective's supreme ability to outfox some of the most cunning members of the criminal fraternity through psycho-analytic detection and ultimately beat them at their own game.

The Secret of the Left-Sided Cipher

Two ghastly murders, the theft of the infamous *Mitra Bhedha* Fortune Diamond, and a secret-coded message believed earmarked for a mysterious underworld criminal band known as the Comrades of the Red Thumb, have Scotland Yard up against a nippy collection of riddles requiring the assistance of London detective Henry von Stray and his able collaborator in the detection of crime Professor John Dilpate. In "The Secret of the Left-Sided Cipher" von Stray and Dilpate find themselves in a high-stakes battle of wits against an ingenious criminal mastermind who just might prove to be their most diabolical adversary yet.

Von Stray and the 290

A simple errand to deliver a sealed letter dating back to the United States Civil War has von Stray and Dilpate looking forward to a relaxing journey to Liverpool until they learn the truth about their mission. The letter was written by a Confederate sea captain whose terrors on the high seas was underwritten by a Liverpool cotton merchant with high-ranking British government contacts reaching all the way to the House of Commons. In "Von Stray and the 290" the 1864 Civil War sea battle between the *U.S.S. Kearsarge* and the *C.S.S. Alabama* off the coast of Cherbourg, France wages on as murder, political scandal, secret societies, Confederate espionage on English soil, and folklore about a lost treasure all resurface at the feet of von Stray and Dilpate more than half a century after the historic sea battle altered the course of the Civil War. Based on actual events, von Stray proves how a page of history can be worth more than a volume of logic when it comes to closing in on a deranged killer.

Also by Andrew and John McAleer

Books by John McAleer

Rex Stout: A Biography (Little, Brown)

Emerson: Days of Encounter (Little, Brown)

Unit Pride (Bantam; Doubleday)

Coign of Vantage (Foul Play Press)

Packed & Loaded: Conversations with James M. Cain with Andrew McAleer (Nimble Books)

Mystery Writing in a Nutshell (with Andrew McAleer) (Rock Publishing)

Books by Andrew McAleer

Edgar and Shamus Go Golden: Twelve Tales of Murder, Mystery, and Master Detection from the Golden Age of Mystery and Beyond,(Down & Out Books, 2022)

Coast to Coast Noir from Sea to Shining Sea, (Down & Out Books, 2020)

Coast to Coast Private Eyes from Sea to Shining Sea, (Down & Out Books, 2017)

Positive Results: True Stories of Inspiration and Hope for Cancer Fighters and Caretakers, (Falconcroft Press, Co., 2017)

Coast to Coast Murder from Sea to Shining Sea, (Down & Out Books, 2015)

A Miscellany of Murder: From the History and Literature to True Crime and Television (Co-author with Stephen D. Rogers; Jim Shannon; Maureen Walsh, and Paula Munier), (Adams Media, 2011)

Fatal Deeds, (Cherokee McGhee, 2011)

Packed & Loaded: *Conversations with James M. Cain,* (Andrew McAleer Compiler; John McAleer Author, Nimble Books, 2010)

The 101 Habits of Highly Successful Novelist: Insider Secrets from Top Writers (Foreword by Bill Pronzini) (Simon & Schuster; Adams Media, 2008)

Mystery Writing in a Nutshell: The World's Most Concise Guide to Mystery and Suspense Writing, (co-author with John McAleer) (Foreword by Edward D. Hoch), Rock Publishing, 2007)

www.ingramcontent.com/pod-product-compliance
Lightning Source LLC
Chambersburg PA
CBHW050333110726
47899CB00007B/2483